# Archie's Way

# Archie's Way

*A Memoir of Craftsmanship and Friendship*

RICHARD EZRA PROBERT

THE LYONS PRESS

Printed in the United States of America

Design by John Gray

10 9 8 7 6 5 4 3 2 1

The Library of Congress Cataloging-in-Publication Data

Probert, Robert Ezra.
    Archie's way: a memoir of craftsmanship and friendship /
  Richard Ezra Probert.
        p.      cm.
    ISBN 1-55821-704-5
    1. Probert, Robert Ezra.    2. Raasch, Archie, 1905–1987.
3. Male friendship—Wisconsin—Ladysmith.    4. Carpenters—
Wisconsin—Ladysmith—Biography.    5. Machinists—Wisconsin—
Ladysmith—Biography.    6. Ladysmith Region (Wis.)—Biography.
I. Title.
CT275.P8494A3    1998
977.5'19—dc21
[B]                                                      98-3149
                                                            CIP

*To Bonnie, Kim, and Jason*

# Contents

# Acknowledgments

In the twenty years since I left Ladysmith, Wisconsin, a day hasn't passed in which I haven't invoked the name of Archie Raasch. He had become so woven into the fabric of my family that it was entirely natural for me to regale a new member to the clan, in this case my son-in-law, Douglas Grad, with story after story about Archie. It was Doug who encouraged me to commit these stories to writing and made sure I got the job done. Thanks, Doug.

Once I began writing in earnest, it became evident that I would need lots of help not only to remember but to remember clearly. Bonnie, my wife during the time I lived in Wisconsin, helped me with both tasks, and I thank her dearly for being with me every step of the way in both the living and the writing. Our children, Kimberly and Jason, eagerly offered their own memories of Archie but didn't stop there. Kimberly, a solid writer in her own right, tirelessly read rewrite after rewrite. Jason joined me on one of my trips to Wisconsin, using camera and sketchbook to help record the visit. This memoir is theirs as well as mine. I couldn't have written this book without them.

To refresh my memory and keep myself honest, I journeyed to Ladysmith twice, where I found many people eager to share their own fond (or not so fond, as the case may be) memories of Archie. In particular, I am indebted to Dick Pedersen, Carol Dauer, Rose Raasch, Alma Edming, Roger Edming, Bill Pfalzgraf, and Ted Felser, each of whom spent many hours talking with me about their recollections of Archie. Whenever I needed to verify a date or address, I counted on Jim Weisenberger, a realtor in Ladysmith who seems to know everybody and every place in the community. Other help came from Paul Bloomberg, Victor Macaruso, Kerm Morgan, Bob Peterson, Bill Fucik, John Terrill, and Melvin Wedwick. I thank Bill and Joanne Chartrand, current owners of Archie's woods, who offered me unlimited access to the woodsy trails and cabin. I also thank Tricia Nolan of the Wisconsin Arts Board, who helped me research some aspects of the book, and Burton Yeagar, for taking the one and only photograph of Archie and me together.

For assistance with technical aspects, I owe a debt of gratitude to all those who willingly shared their knowledge and expertise, especially: Ron Lavoie, President of Homer America; Dr. R. Bruce Hoadley, Professor of Forestry at the University of Massachusetts, Amherst; Steven Quail of Delta International Machinery; Hardy Thomisik of Star Tools; Bernie DiDuro, Business Representative, International Association of Machinists, District 6; my friends at Badge Machine; Dan Swain of Swain Technologies; Jeff Huff, President of Huff Equipment, and his employees Rick Frost and Chris Weber; John Probert, my brother, an expert on Model A Fords; Barry G. Schuler, retired President of The Williamson Free School of Mechanical Trades; Aldren Watson, expert on hand tools; Dominic Fornato, Sergeant, Patrol Division of Jeddo Highland Coal Company; Wendell Smith of the Rochester Woodworkers Society; David Schmitz, Rochester Institute of Technology; and Tami Creech, Midwestern Climate Center.

I owe special thanks to Claudia Hornby, friend and writer, who was always available by e-mail to help knock writer's block out of the way; also, to my brother, Carl Probert, for helping me recall some scenes from childhood; and to friend and counselor Stanley Lieberfruend, for unwavering support.

To master machinist and friend Gerry Gooley, I pay special tribute for taking me into his shop and helping me recall the awe of working with machine tools, as well as providing me access to his sizable library. Gerry is a machinist's machinist.

Joining the early believers in the book, I thank John Talbot, my agent, whose tenacity led me to my association with the good folks at The Lyons Press. I express my deepest gratitude to Senior Editor, Bryan Oettel, whose expert guidance, patience, and gentle commands were key factors in my bringing this book to fruition.

Finally, I thank Carmelita Britton, my partner, friend, and confidante, who lived with me through all the trials and tribulations, and there were many, associated with writing this book. Thanks, Britt.

# Introduction

"Feel the wood," my grandfather instructed me. "Use the tips of your fingers. When you feel a bump or a dip, you know you've got more work to do. Here, let me show you," he said, reaching for a Stanley No. 80 wood scraper. A few steady pulls and feather-light, translucent ribbons of wood fell to the side. "Now, here, let your fingers run over it. See? Nice and smooth." It was the summer of 1950. I was eight years old.

Craftsmanship was honored in my extended family. Grandpa insisted on it. My father did, too, but not with objects. For him, it was musicianship, particularly as it applies to singing. Where Grandpa emoted over nicely fitted drawers, Dad got goose pimples over well-sung high notes. Grandpa made things, Dad made music. I did both, and while I decided on a career in teaching and performing music, I was never without a shop or a project to keep my hands and tools busy.

With the exception of my college years, Grandpa, Dad, and their craftsmen or musical cronies were readily accessible to me, helping me to balance my life between making music and making things. Then, in 1972, Hurricane Agnes abruptly sent her rushing muddy waters down Pennsylvania's Susquehanna River, through Wyoming Valley into my basement shop, up the basement stairs and through my just finished restoration of a turn-of-the-century townhouse. The devastation was complete. Warped wood, scarred tools, marred finishes, and twisted beams turned my love of working with my hands to bitterness. I fixed up the house, sold it, resigned my position as a music teacher at a local college, and, within a year, moved my young family a thousand miles away to the northern Wisconsin community of Ladysmith. Joining the faculty of a small liberal arts college, I bought a brand-new house with no desire to have a shop or unpack any of my rust-stained tools. I had had enough of hands-on work.

I survived my first cold, snowy year in northern Wisconsin by immersing myself in teaching and performing, and for a small town, Ladysmith had plenty of talent to draw upon. But as winter wore on, I felt less and less complete. My withdrawal from hands-on work bothered me. I missed machinists and cabinetmakers, lumbermen and hardware stores. I longed to hear and be involved in shoptalk, that universal language men use when working on projects together. I missed learning new tricks from old craftsmen and making things. I missed seeing something emerge from a plank of wood or a block of steel.

With the arrival of spring—in northern Wisconsin that means late April—I met a man who would help me make things right. Archie Raasch was a seventy-four-year-old machinist whose life revolved around a machine shop that he built behind his house, and an 800-acre tract of woods that he and his friend Harry Pedersen owned twenty-five miles north of town. Archie worked alone. His shop was his domain, his place, his signature. Archie did things his way, with purpose and precision, and he did it in the solitary comfort of his shop. Archie was a private man, mysterious. He was also extremely talented, perhaps even a genius. From the moment I walked into his dimly lit shop and smelled the pungent odor of machine cutting oil, I knew I was in a special place.

The essential ingredient of our developing friendship was my working in his shop. To be sure, my first Saturday morning in Archie's shop was a humbling experience, but in time, working alongside Archie came to be about more than making things. It was master and apprentice, craftsman and artist, old man and young man, in which learning about life and friendship were key elements in every project. When I confessed my love of working with wood over machining steel, Archie led me to his garage, where behind a large sliding door he had a fully equipped woodshop.

As Archie and I came to know each other and trust in each other's work, our shop activity extended into a deep and abiding friendship, but it took work and understanding to get there. As open as I was to establishing a friendship, Archie was guarded. I was confused over his reticence to go beyond shoptalk, and his constant badgering about my being a teacher was grating on my nerves. Following an argument that nearly led to our going separate ways, first Archie's wife, Lillian, and then, a few months later, Archie himself revealed a tightly held secret that he had kept hidden through his entire life. With his disclosure our friendship deepened, and as with a great deal in our relationship, my horizons were broadened. Our Saturday mornings in the shop expanded to include hunting, fishing, and driving back roads to visit some of his old friends that he hadn't seen in years. My family joined Archie and Lillian in driving one of his three antique cars in local parades. We cross-country skied on trails that he had carefully cut through his woods and visited his warm cabin on cold Wisconsin Sunday afternoons to play checkers and chat. Archie became eager to share his knowledge about nature with my children, Kimberly and Jason, often walking hand-in-hand with them down one or another of his wooded trails in search of hazelnuts, lichen shelves, and beaver cuttings.

In 1979, I moved to Ohio, where I had accepted an administrative and faculty position at a prestigious private college. My parting with Archie was sad and very difficult. Attempts to remain friends by phone, letters, and an occasional visit fell short. Within a few years after leaving Wisconsin, I returned to Ladysmith, at Lillian's request, to be with her for Archie's funeral.

# Archie's Way

# *Prologue*

High in the hills of the anthracite coal belt of eastern Pennsylvania, my hometown of Hazleton was a breeding ground for traditional work ethics and family values. Each had its place in my childhood, but not in direct association with the brutal life of the coal miner. My childhood was rooted in craftsmanship and art.

Every Sunday at dinnertime, my grandfather, as patriarch of our extended family, sat at the head of the table that he made from quartersawn oak. He made the twelve chairs that were filled with family and friends. He made a matching china cabinet, a buffet with a beveled mirror backsplash, and a side table with drawers and a shelf underneath to hold a chest full of gleaming silverware. He had inlaid a pattern of ebony, ash, walnut, and cherry around the apron of the table, drawer fronts, and door frames.

As a young child, I found delight in reaching under the thick linen tablecloth to feel the satiny finish of the wood underneath. I remember my fingers caressing the side of my chair where they found the right rear tapered leg and went as far as they could, downward along its subtle, smooth curve. Standing in front of the tall glass doors of the china cabinet catching the gossamer reflection of my young image mixing with the wonders of a woodworker's art, I marveled at my grandfather's craftsmanship, sure that someday, I would do the same.

Grandpa was born of an age when hands and mind worked in consort to build and repair the day-to-day objects of life and family. Located in the basement of his home, his shop was an inseparable part of his daily life. I was always welcome to join him there where, it seemed to me, our relationship was quiet and special. I don't remember being treated as a child when I worked with him; rather, I remember us talking about wood, tools, thought, and work, as if together they were what life was all about.

Grandpa's livelihood as a vocational arts teacher afforded me opportunities to visit other shops, from small, one-bench wood-shops to massive foundries where cascades of menacing sparks flew through dusky, ill-lit cavernous buildings. My interests in woodwork expanded to include metalwork, welding, forging, and machining steel. Through Grandpa, I met one craftsman after another, each having his own stories to tell, his own well-guarded tricks of the trade. Returning vets from the Korean War filled Grandpa's evening classes, and I took advantage of being a young boy amid young, experienced men. I loved being around them, many of whom took the time to teach me tricks of the trade, and even though I had learned many of these tricks from my grandfather, I savored my time with these young men. They shared with me food from their lunch boxes and talked about Europe and Korea, deer hunting, and women. They told me of war but spared me the details. One fellow taught me to play the harmonica, then gave me one. I still have it and I can still play the "Clarinet Polka," a song he taught to me nearly fifty years ago.

Around the same time that I was working on projects with Grandpa and spending time with his "boys," as Grandpa called his students, my father took me to a concert in Weatherly, Pennsylvania, a small hillside town not far from our hometown of Hazleton. Around the altar of a small church, a chorus of men assembled to regale their eager audience with songs of their trade—mining songs. I recall this concert as the first time I felt the majesty and power of choral music. Their opening hymn, "Abide with Me," astonished me, and somewhere in my young mind a union between making things and making music was formed. My father introduced me to the voices of Jussi Bjoerling, Thomas L. Thomas, Lily Pons, Paul Robeson, Ezio Pinza, and Fyodor Chaliapin. I loved Lawrence Tibbett's recording of Mussorgsky's "Song of the Flea." On Saturday afternoons, our house was filled with the strong, sweet sounds of opera courtesy of the Texaco Metropolitan Opera broadcasts, and each week I looked forward to the Firestone Hour with Charles Vorhees and the Firestone Orchestra. Whenever I had the opportunity, I sang. Once I sang "Sixteen Tons," a song made popular during the 1950s by Tennessee Ernie Ford. I let it fly during a sixth grade class devoted to the history of coal mining. I just sat at my desk and began singing. Much to her credit, my teacher, Miss Cauley, let me sing and when I was finished, commended me with, "You sing just like your father."

When in the eighth grade it came time for me to select a course of study for my high school years, my argument to combine singing with cabinetmaking fell on deaf ears. Whereas I saw the two endeavors as closely allied, my school system saw them as incompatible. If I were to indulge my passion for music, I would be required to enter the academic program, which I did, reasoning that my grandfather's shop was readily available to me for evening and weekend woodworking.

My high school grades hovering in the C's, it was my singing voice and a benevolent admissions director that opened my way to college and beyond. What followed was marriage in my senior year, graduate school, teaching music to grades six through twelve, the birth of a daughter, a National Teaching Fellowship in Music appointment at Juniata College, then a triumphant return to the eastern Pennsylvania coal fields to join the faculty of my undergraduate school, Wilkes University. A full circle. Back to family and friends. Grandpa's shop. In time for my father's death.

We soon became the second owners of a three-story brick townhouse with a slate-covered Dutch gambrel roof that was built at the turn of the century in Wilkes-Barre, Pennsylvania. It was filled with wonders of a bygone age: original wallpapered walls, varnished oak woodwork, perfect floors, red-and-amber colored glass and brass shaded gaslights (disconnected), an old kitchen, new boiler, marginal electric power, a large claw-footed porcelain tub, no shower, finished attic, dry basement, front porch, back porch, second-story back porch, bay windows in the living room and master bedroom, bench seat in the dining room with a three-inch plate rack all around and an exposed oak-beamed ceiling. A tiny yard and a one-stall garage finished the property. We restored, refinished, rewired. We also remodeled, but just the old kitchen. I made period-style birch cabinets.

With another child on the way, life seemed complete—all we had to do was live it. I celebrated my thirtieth birthday in June 1972. One week later, Hurricane Agnes turned the normally placid Susquehanna River into a raging torrent of destruction. Our house filled with muddy water right to the ceiling of the first floor.

Our restoration was for naught. Doors swelled, never to open again, pocket doors warped inside the walls, floors heaved, and after more than a half century, the wallpaper peeled. Our new

Steinway, twisted and broken, was destroyed. A fireman who had just completed pumping water from my basement caught me crying as I looked over what once was my shop.

Cleaning up and getting things back into shape was, thankfully, as much therapy as it was work. Otherwise, I'm sure that the searing shock and dull ache of the flood's aftermath would have overwhelmed me. As it was, with lots of help from the federal government, friends and family and the Red Cross, we moved back into the house in September, just in time for the birth of our son, Jason.

Our lives adjusted. Postdisaster depression flowed in and out of our daily routine, but slowly, chinks of light found their way through our gray pall. We were young. I was a college music teacher; my wife Bonnie, a skilled registered nurse. We could go anywhere. It was time to move on.

# 1 · The Shop

*His life, full as it was of industry, was like a combination of carefully thought out details in a predetermined progressive tolerance.*

Torsten K. W. Althin, C. E. Johansson—*The Master of Measurement*, 1948

By the time I moved to Ladysmith, not including graduate school, I had lived in three different states. Changing jobs and places were, I suppose, a part of my generation. Moving about meant advancement and, in my case, Hurricane Agnes notwithstanding, that's certainly what happened. A peripatetic lifestyle, however, didn't lead to establishing close friends, and that bothered me, especially finding friends who were also craftsmen. But it did give me an opportunity to sniff around new places, explore new things, and whenever the fancy struck me, I would do just that by packing my family in the car and driving down unfamiliar roads. One of my favorite rides during my first year in Ladysmith was down along County Road J. I wasn't sure where the rest of the alphabetized roads were, but I knew that J would lead us down a particularly scenic route along the Flambeau River. Dammed above and below town, the river ran quiet and on a sunny day was a mirrored ribbon reflecting the fields and woods that ran to its banks. My first winter in northern Wisconsin had been long, longer than any winter I could remember, and cabin fever, a malady of the north country, certainly had a grip on me. Then, on one particular day, the sun was out, and I hoped that its heat would finally melt what few remaining mounds of dirty snow lingered about, mostly in shaded areas. On my drives down County J, I had noticed a neat yellow-framed ranch house that sat on a corner property where a road that ran off to one or another farms intersected with County J. What caught my eye about the place was its purposeful look, its clean-cut lawn and growth of mature trees that blocked northern winds. Facing due south, the front of the house had large windows ready to capture every warming ray the sun could give.

As we drove past the house, I glanced at the property. This time my eye caught a sight that warmed my cabin-fevered heart. Two beautifully restored Model A's sat posed like a couple for a daguerreotype, immovable, yet projecting a serene sense of time and place. I sat antsy in my car wanting to drive up close to the cars to make their acquaintance. "Beautiful," I heard myself say to no one in particular. "Look at those Model A's. Damn, just look at those cars." I slowed to a stop.

"Dad, what's a Model A?" Kimberly, my six-year-old daughter asked, no doubt feeling my wonder over it all.

"What's a Model A?" mimicked her eighteen-month-old brother, Jason.

"A car. An old car that sounds like music," I said rhapsodically, as I slowly made my way up the driveway.

"Are you sure you should be doing this?" cautioned Bonnie.

Remembering my grandfather's words, *When you admire something, go find the person that made it,* I answered assuredly, "I'm sure."

As if on cue, a man came out of the side door of the house. He was broadly built and looked like the first five feet, ten inches, of the Washington Monument. My eyes diverted to his; he gave me a subtle nod. I continued up the driveway.

As if stage-directed, the man went from the side door of his house, disappeared momentarily behind the car that was to my left, and emerged, proudly framing himself between the two icons of a bygone era. He gave me another nod. I stepped confidently from my car. Bonnie, Kim, and Jason remained seated.

This business about interpreting another's nod, which I ascribe more to men than women, was something I became accustomed to when I was a youngster. I discovered that whenever I visited a shop, if I stood quietly enough and made eye contact with a fellow, then slightly nodded, more often than not I would get a nod in return. Once the nodding ritual was complete, I felt that it was okay to approach.

Dressed in a pressed flannel shirt and green work clothes, his pants held up by wide tan suspenders that had a blue stripe down the middle, the man gave me the impression of a no-nonsense sort of fellow with a lot of muscle. His hands and feet appeared exaggerated, oversized, emphasized to show strength similar, I thought, to a Rodin sculpture. Grayish blue eyes looked warmly through a pair of half plastic, half metal–framed glasses. Large ears accentuated his strong face. His square jaw was relaxed. No smile appeared on his face, but he wasn't scowling either.

"Well, what are you going to do?" the man said directly. "Let those kids out of the car, you can't keep them locked up forever, you know. My name's Archie Raasch, what's yours?" he asked, without offering to shake my hand.

"Richard," I answered, as I motioned for Bonnie and the kids to get out of the car.

Archie was seventy years old when I met him standing between his matched set of Model A's. He reminded me of my grandfather and other men of his time—strong men who took enormous pride in their work. Looking at the cars, and then at Archie, it was apparent that these Fords were not simply show-pieces but testaments to the skill of a real craftsman. It was thrilling, but I contained my enthusiasm, lest I appear patronizing. I had been around enough craftsmen to know that any show of arrogance would have me and my family back in the car and on our way. Rather than speaking, I stood doing what came naturally, drooling over the cars.

"What kind of car you have there? Foreign, isn't it?" Archie asked in clipped tones.

"From Sweden. But," I added as a mild disclaimer, "with a family, I want the safest car I can get."

"Well, that's something, I guess," Archie replied matter-of-factly.

He was sizing me up, as I was him—a different sizing up than I was accustomed to in the college crowd, where newly made acquaintances talk of academe and drop names, usually accompanied by "Did you read the latest . . .?" I knew that with Archie, sizing up would be a matter of little talk and lots of proof. There would be no bullshit spoken here, of that I was certain.

The classic Model A's were a matched pair, both bodies painted beige with dark brown trim. The fenders were a deep, solid black that reflected in odd contours, puffy white clouds drifting in a blue sky. One of the cars was a two-door sedan designed to keep its four passengers comfortably out of wind and rain. The other was a coupe with its romantic rumble seat open to the world. I thought of my father's tales of wooing my mother in one of them. Dad's spirit clicked its heels. Each Ford had chrome-plated spring steel bumpers and shiny black rubber-covered running boards that ran from front fender to back fender, ready to assist driver and passenger into their high cabin seats. On the top of the right rear bumper of the coupe, a zinc foot pad with an identical one positioned on the right rear fender helped passengers into and out of the rumble seat. A black, long-grained simulated-leather cover with the FORD logo neatly embossed in the center covered the spare tire that hung at the rear of the sedan. A wood and chrome folding trunk rack completed the back of the coupe.

Clearly in his element, Archie proceeded to give me and my family a tour—and by his methodical approach, a well-seasoned tour—of his Model A's by walking us slowly and silently around each car. By monitoring our admiration in the form of "oohs" and "ahhs," Archie would soon know whether our appreciation for classic beauty was either passionate or polite.

Rather than ask questions, I let my body language, which consisted of bending and leaning, nodding affirmatively and smiling, do the talking. I carefully studied the curved fenders, gleaming headlamps, square radiators, and inviting cabins. Archie's penchant for perfection was everywhere, down to the smallest detail. My reverence for his work and Henry Ford's genius was suddenly interrupted by my daughter Kim. "Can we sit in the rumble seat?" she requested, including her brother Jason. Archie replied by reaching out his strong arms, lifting first Kim and then Jason to the honored place. They were smiling.

With the children safely seated in the high open rumble seat, Archie, still silent, opened the driver's side doorway of the coupé, looked at me, and nodded. I climbed behind the massive black Bakelite steering wheel, which had a small black horn button in the center of its hub. (It took considerable discipline not to push that button.) A small metal tab attached to a narrow rim just below the horn button activated the headlights. Small levers, similar to turn signal levers, jutted from both sides of the steering column. Seeing me eyeing the levers, Archie broke his silence. "The left one adjusts the spark, the other is the throttle. Putting the spark lever up"—he reached in and moved the lever to its uppermost position—"retards the spark so the plug fires when the cylinder reaches top-dead-center. You need that to start it up." Then pushing the lever down, he noted, "But to run right you move the lever all the way down. That sets the spark to fire early. Today, it's all automatic." Reaching in front of me and across the steering wheel, Archie touched the other lever. "This is the throttle—does the same thing as the gas pedal only it's up here when you need it."

With that, Archie withdrew his arm from the cabin and from directly in front of me. I sat astonished that, after his quiet spell, he opened up his own throttle, spewing out all sorts of information. Just like Grandpa's boys, I thought. The whole scene with his lecture and demonstration took less than a few minutes but its significance was gratifying.

Although I had developed some good friendships at the college as well as with some town folks, I still felt something of a void. Already, from this brief meeting, I had a special feeling about Archie and I was hopeful that a friendship with him would help take care of that.

"That's the gear shift. You know they didn't have automatics back then." Eyeing my Volvo, he asked with a light shade of sarcasm, "Do you know how to drive a standard transmission?"

Hoping that his question was leading to his inviting me to drive the car, I answered with a bit more youthful enthusiasm than the moment called for. "Sure I do. My father made me learn on a standard. I prefer it, actually."

His reply of "You do, do you?" was followed by, "Jump out, I'll start the engine." Buoyed by the possibility that, indeed, I might get to drive the car, I slid effortlessly and quickly from the seat. As I touched the running board with my feet, Archie moved aside to ceremoniously lift the hood. It may not be a great moment to some, but for me, the raising of a car hood is a dramatic event that requires a touch of reverence. The heart of any car is the engine, and no matter how well-kept or shiny it may be on the outside, it is the engine compartment that separates the men from the boys.

Releasing two spring-loaded catches that held the side-opening hood in place, Archie gave the moment all it was worth. Delighted to be the audience for his command performance, I stood eagerly to one side. As he slowly raised the louvered hood, the bright Wisconsin sun lit up the engine compartment to reveal a small, impeccably clean, green-painted four-cylinder flathead engine. The engine compartment was as striking in its simplicity as today's engine compartments are intimidating in their complexity. Archie turned to look at me. I was enraptured, and he knew it.

As I stretched to get a closer look at the details, Archie lifted himself behind the wheel. "Stand clear," he called out, causing me to step back. I watched as he adjusted the spark and throttle levers to their optimum setting. Leaning slightly forward, he deftly turned on the ignition. Pushing a small, floor-mounted, metal button with his foot, he activated the starter. The small engine that powered America into the automobile age came to life.

Once running, Archie left the spark fully retarded, adjusted the throttle, and tuned the sound of the Model A with the same care with which a concertmaster tunes an orchestra.

The unique sound of the Model A's engine emerged as he set the idle so low that I could hear each cylinder fire in turn. The kids, who had been enjoying their flight through fancy in the rumble seat, hushed to quietness. Staccato bursts of the exhaust accompanied the subtle whirl of a smooth turning crankshaft, camshaft, and flywheel. Unfiltered air rushed into the open throat of the carburetor, producing a delicate hissing background to this mechanical chamber music—a Bach suite transcribed for four cylinders, whirling fan, and popping valves. I was certain that for the first time in their young lives, my children felt the awe that comes with being so intimately connected to the subtle workings of a machine and that was what accounted for their stillness.

Breaking the human silence, a woman came out of the house's side door with a comment my family and I were longing to hear: "Archie, why don't you take them for a ride?" Leaving the motor performing its playful tune, Archie jumped from the driver's seat and relatched the louvered hood. I helped Bonnie climb into the rumble seat, where she sat with Jason on her lap, giggling in anticipation. I climbed into the passenger seat ready for a memory-building ride.

Archie introduced the friendly and thoughtful woman "my wife, Lillian." We all smiled and said a quick hello while Archie climbed behind the simple console of the old Ford.

"You folks enjoy your ride," Lillian sang out as she closed the driver's-side door, looking fondly at Archie, knowing that our first ride was as much his pleasure as ours.

County Road J took on a new meaning as the Model A transported us back to a simpler time. The Flambeau River danced. Archie was quiet, hunched behind the steering wheel with his large hands clasping the wheel at the ten and two o'clock positions, swaying and moving in tandem with his roadworthy Ford. Expressing his contentment, Archie pushed the black horn button in the middle of the steering wheel. The low, distinctive, guttural *aaoogah* rattling from the Model A's horn announced his and our pleasure to the world. Kim and Jason screamed and giggled with delight. The hop of the Model A, the delight of my children, and the old man hunched over the big black steering wheel had a comfortable feel to it. Feeling relaxed, I looked over at Archie and asked, "Did you do the restoration?"

"Yup," he answered in a flat tone that caught me by surprise. I had expected more enthusiasm, perhaps even prideful response.

"You sure did a great job."

"Yup."

"Were you able to get parts, are they still available?"

"Yup."

Attempting to get Archie into a conversation, I asked, "How long did it take you to finish the job?"

"Long enough," Archie responded with a tone of voice that signaled the end of the conversation.

I wondered why he was so terse, but decided not to push. A few quiet moments passed, then suddenly, Archie interrupted by asking sardonically, "When is the last time you restored a Model A?" I guess that I could have interpreted his response as a joke, even a poor one, but this was no joke. Archie meant what he said and I took it seriously.

Startled, I asked, "What do you mean?"

"If you didn't restore one, how do you know I did a good job?" he challenged.

The moment was uncomfortable and awkward, especially given the confined space of the Model A and the newness of our acquaintance. Nevertheless, I was not about to allow Archie to question my sincerity or my seasoned eye for quality work. "I know good work when I see it and hear it and touch it. This is good work. I'm just admiring it," I responded.

Archie chose silence accompanied by a passive look that gave no indication of the nature of my offense or his reaction to my rebuttal. I reasoned that Archie interpreted my compliment as condescending—if I myself did not experience hands-on work, how could I appreciate what went into the restoration of the Fords? As it was, I had plenty of experience to build upon, but how was Archie to know? I decided to dismiss this uncomfortable moment, remain quiet, and enjoy the ride.

Our excursion into yesteryear soon ended, as Archie turned into his driveway and backed up next to the companion car. With a smooth reach and turn of the ignition key, Archie stopped the engine, which chugged to silence.

Looking over to me without a hint of irritation, he surprised me by asking, "Do you want to see my shop?"

My heart leapt. First of all, the invitation would never have come had Archie suspected that I would not appreciate his place of work, of that I was sure. I also suspected that Archie's shop, like the shops of most craftsmen, would say more about the man than I could ever glean from talking. His shop would be a window into what made him tick and I was eager to look through it. There was no getting around it: I needed an Archie in my life. Pure and simple, without balancing the world of musicmaking with the world of craftsmen, my life wobbled. As these thoughts zipped through my mind, I heard myself bubble forth with clipped, excited bits. "You bet. I sure would. Can I see it now? I've got the time. Where is your shop?"

"Well, come on then," Archie interrupted my dribble. "Let's get those kids of yours out of the rumble seat."

Lillian had heard us coming up the driveway and was already out of the house. "I'm going to show Deek my shop."

*Deek?* I thought that I had introduced myself as Richard. What was this *Deek* business? I had been trying to get people to call me Richard for years, so I was sensitive to being called Dick, which Archie obviously pronounced Deek. Not the time or place, I thought, to make any corrections. Maybe later. Maybe never.

Lillian stepped right in, knowing full well the import of Archie showing his shop to a stranger, and led Bonnie and the kids to the back yard.

"You're new to town, Deek?" Archie observed as my family and Lillian disappeared around the garage. "Live up where County Road J takes a turn to town, do you?"

Observant fellow, I thought. Nodding, I offered, "I'm teaching at the college."

His forehead slightly wrinkled, he asked pointedly, "Teacher?"

"Music! I teach music. Singing."

"People need to learn to do that?" he asked instantly with a note of sarcasm.

"Some people do. Do you sing?" It was asked innocently, but without uttering any response whatsoever, Archie turned and headed up a small road that cut around the right side of the garage. I knew not to pursue this conversation.

Walking to his left, I lagged just slightly behind to get his sense of direction. He had a determined way of walking: hands clasped behind his back; shoulders slightly arched forward; head slightly lifted to offset the angle of his shoulders; one large, leather workbooted foot placed in front of the other; a steady, heavy, self-assured pace.

Heading up the lane, we entered a different world. None of the structures that came slowly into view were visible from the front of the house and garage. In striking contrast to the soft, yellow clapboard–sided house and garage, we were entering Archie's world, which I likened to a miniature version of an industrial complex. The main structure, which I took to be his shop, was surrounded by smaller buildings, some no larger than a shack. The buildings were covered with tar paper held securely in place with equally spaced vertical lengths of lath. On the sides of two of the three smaller structures, Archie had fashioned shed roofs that jutted from their sides and were held up with rough-cut poles. Under these roofs, ten or more face cords of cut and split firewood were neatly stacked, seasoning in the open air. Leading me past one of the sheds, Archie offered, "There's enough parts in there to build a few more Model A's." Then, moving quickly to the next shed, he unlocked and opened the door. "Take a look in here," Archie commanded. "You ever see the likes of these?" Inside were two rows of perfectly restored antique engines, some painted red, some green, all having decorative gold pinstriping. "I restored every one," he said, looking me squarely in the eye. "See the one near the back. It's from back in nineteen-twelve," he said with boyish pleasure while pointing to a one-cylinder engine with a shiny, exposed, overhead camshaft and large, heavy, cast-iron flywheel. He reverently closed and safely locked up the shed.

As we walked past the third shack, his step quickened and he made no mention of what may lie behind its doors. My curiosity piqued, I wanted to ask, but holding myself in check, I followed Archie, who continued his hurried step past the large shop building to a three-stall garage. "Here's where I keep the Fords," Archie said.

I was busting to see the shop, but knew I had to be patient.

"Why three stalls, Archie, is there another Model A in there?"

"Nope, two Fords are enough for anybody."

Walking to wood-framed, sheet metal–paneled doors of the stall farthest to the left, he unlocked a padlock, lifted a sturdy iron bar, and swung open the two opposing doors to reveal the high, back end of a 1927 REO Flying Cloud. "Here, take a look at this," Archie said, pointing to a colorful display ad that he had taped to the back side of one of the doors. It was an ad for the REO that was identified as coming from the June 25, 1927, edition of the *Saturday Evening Post*. "Go ahead, teacher, give it a read." Then, in the same tone of voice he had used when he challenged me during the ride in the Model A, he added, "You might learn something." I pushed his comment aside and read aloud:

> *Take the wheel of a Reo Flying Cloud, point her prow toward the land of beyond, sail across wide valleys and over the challenging hills, and then you'll understand the fitness of her name.*
>
> *You'll know why Reo christened her in honor of the most famous of the world's most beautiful means of travel, the clipper ship* Flying Cloud.
>
> *You'll learn from her easy, effortless flight, her floating comfort, how like your dreams of drifting in a summer cloud, travel can be.*
>
> *As the years roll by, and your Flying Cloud remains eager, alert, alive, you'll be increasingly glad that you possess one of the finest, fastest models of America's Longest Lasting Car.*
>
> *"Sail" one today. Then you'll understand why she is called "Flying Cloud."*

"Car ads never change, do they, Archie?" I observed.

"Guess not. Now how about we take a look at the shop." I helped Archie close the garage doors behind the REO. Lowering the iron bar, he set the padlock and slowly walked over to the largest building in the complex. Facing due east, an afternoon shadow shaded the front of the rectangular shop building, which had a high peaked roof topped with corrugated tin. To the left was a door and a small window. The remainder of the front of the heavily built structure was a commercial-size garage with a large, high, bi-fold paneled door covering the opening.

Sensing my eagerness, Archie took his time unlocking the impressive, well-worn Master padlock. He then slung aside the heavy iron hasp as though he were opening a bank vault and stepped into the dark void. I followed and stood just inside of the door.

The shop was dimly lit, cool, and smelled like work: pungent, serious, earthy, threatening. The distinct odor of machine cutting oil flushed pleasant childhood memories from my mind's lockers. I may as well have been nine years old on a shop visit with Grandpa rather than being thirty-one years old in the presence of a seasoned machinist. The aroma of machine cutting oil, which comes from a mixture of derivatives from processed petroleum products and animal fat, permeated the air with a smell similar to a very hot, cast-iron frying pan, and I was delighted to once again experience its power.

My eyes slowly adjusted from the bright Wisconsin day to the incandescent light cast from porcelain enameled shades that hung high from the ceiling. Archie's shop emerged from dull light like a stage set being slowly backlit behind a scrim.

My first impression was one of warmth. Everything seemed to be worn at about the same rate—similar to being in an old person's house where the furniture and setting had a patina, where no reason needs to be given for the look of things. I felt peace in this shop, as if it were a place made holy by all that went on there. Details faded into a kaleidoscope of geometric shapes, muted grays and greens, rough and smooth textures. As if from a lifting fog, details emerged. I looked at Archie. He belonged here, the same way he belonged sitting behind the wheel of his beloved Ford. His hands, which seemed so large in the out-of-doors, were in proportion to the large, heavy shapes of the machinery. Without moving my body, I turned my head to see a small lathe standing on patterned, open cast-iron legs, which were more substantial than, but similar to, the iron ends of a park bench. I took a few steps toward the machine. "You like that lathe, Deek?" Archie inquired with a friendly voice.

"My grandfather had one just like it," I said, reaching out my left hand to touch the wide, worn leather drive belt that ran from the machine's heavy steel cone pulley to a device I took to be a gear reduction case, then to a large electric motor that hung from the back of the lathe.

"Oh, he did, did he," Archie said, as if I had in some way challenged him. My curious reaction to his comment was satisfied when he added, "I never knew mine." It was a personal comment, the first that he had offered me, and I felt the mollifying pull of compatibility.

I raised my eyes to scan the forty-foot wall that ran along the south side of the shop, which, unlike that of his house, was windowless. "What's in all of those boxes, Archie?" I asked, referring to hundreds of cigar boxes, tin boxes, wooden boxes, and cans of all sizes that sat on five rows of shelves held to the wall with heavy steel brackets.

"Lots of stuff," Archie replied, appearing delighted that I asked but leaving my question hanging in the air. Feeling more at home, I took the liberty to take the lead and, walking around the little lathe that I had just admired, strolled part way down the wall. I stopped by two beautifully crafted oak chests with carefully fitted finger-jointed corners.

"What 'stuff' are in these?"

Archie came hurriedly up alongside me, protectively separating me from the chests. "These are my special tools." Dropping the front of the box and sliding it under a fitted slot in the bottom of the chest, Archie delicately opened one of the six shallow drawers, his index fingers and thumbs clasping two small brass knobs attached to each side of the drawer front. "Here, take a look," he said, stepping aside with pride.

I had the feeling of looking into a jewelry box. Lined with dark green felt, the drawer was full of small gleaming tools and gauges. Steel scales of various lengths and calibrations shared the drawer with feeler gauges, screw thread pitch gauges, and adjustable depth gauges. One by one, Archie opened and closed each close-fitted drawer, displaying his prized tools. With obvious delight, he showed me various-size micrometers, many sizes and shapes of calipers, dial indicators, telescoping gauges, numerous punches, scribes, and many tools that I could not identify.

Carefully sliding the cover from its pocket at the base of the cabinet, Archie closed and latched the cover over the front of the chest.

"Now, I don't show these to many people," he said, reaching for a wooden case that sat on a shelf below. The superbly crafted case was maybe three inches thick and appeared to be made of mahogany. Undoing a catch, he raised the lid.

"What are these, Archie?" I asked intently, referring to neat rows of various-size steel blocks.

"Jo blocks, Deek. See this?" Archie said, lifting a block from the case. "This is exactly one inch, no more and no less, that is at sixty-eight degrees."

Holding out my hand, "May I? Why sixty-eight degrees?"

"Nature," he said, slightly shaking his head as if I should know the answer. Offering me the block as if it were a precious jewel, he admonished, "Don't drop it."

The block felt heavy for its size, as if made of gold. Its corners were crisp, its edges polished to a high sheen. As I turned the block over in my hands, Archie proceeded to answer my question. "Standard measure, Deek. Without a standard of measure, and I mean to the millionth of an inch, there was no accurate way to make duplicate parts. Without Johansson, the industrial revolution wouldn't have happened. Old Henry Ford couldn't have gotten anywhere making those Model A's without them. Standard measure, Deek, the heart of everything that goes on in this shop and every shop worth anything."

"Here, let me show you," he said, continuing his lesson. He took the one-inch block from my hand, took another from the box, and twisted the two pieces together. "Okay, Deek, pull them apart," he directed me. I took the blocks from Archie's outstretched hand and sure enough, they held fast.

"Must be vacuum, Archie. They're stuck fast."

"Nope. Molecules, Deek," he said, through an excited chuckle. "Molecules," he repeated emphatically. "Vacuum you can only get fourteen pounds. There's a lot more going on than that. Old Johansson polished these blocks to a point where the molecules bind when you put them together. It's called wringing. Didn't they teach you anything in those schools you went to?" he said with a slightly mocking tone.

"No, Archie, I guess they didn't. Jo blocks never came up in music school."

"Well, fancy that."

"How did you learn it all, Archie? In school?" I asked innocently.

His voice was raised as he said, "Deek, I'd rather play piano in a whorehouse than get caught in some school. I learned the way I learned it, and that's all there is to it." His tone caught me short. I stood silently, a bit shaken, as Archie put the precious box of Jo blocks back on the shelf and walked over to the large lathe. Then, as it had during our drive when I queried him about the restoration of the Fords, his voice calmed.

"Come over here, Deek," he commanded, but in a friendlier tone of voice that relieved my anxiety. "This is where I do most of my work. This lathe and I have been together for many years."

"How many, Archie?" I asked.

"Many," he said flatly, as he continued to guide me around his shop.

Opposite the front of the large lathe was a heavy bench supported by two columns of oak drawers that ran from the floor to the bench top. "Here, take a look," Archie said, as he opened and closed each drawer in rapid succession. My eyes caught glitters from hundreds of drill bits, cutting tools of all sizes and shapes, taps and dies, knurling tools, screw-cutting jigs, and specialty attachments for the lathe. The sullen, dark shadows of emery and polishing cloth sharing a drawer with red sticks of cutting rouge gave the appearance of a theatrical makeup kit.

Above the bench hung pipe wrenches, combination wrenches, adjustable angle wrenches, gear pullers, and C-clamps. Chisels, punches, number and letter stamping sets, and a brass hammer sat on a sturdy shelf. Two handheld hacksaws hung from pieces of curved flat iron screwed to the side of the bench. Overhead hung a five-horsepower air compressor that was suspended from the ceiling by heavy iron strapping bolted firmly to a steel I beam.

On the left side of the bench top, Archie had fashioned a holder for the tools he most commonly used when working at the lathe. Live and dead centers, collets, a four-jaw chuck and key, a faceplate, straight, right- and left-angled cutting tool holders, boring tools, countersinks, center drills, and a common lathe dog.

As I turned to walk back to the front of the shop, Archie caught me looking quizzically at the massive oak-paneled doors that covered the large garage-size door opening that I had noticed on the front of the shop. "I got those from a church that was doing some renovation. They used to divide a room in half. Imagine. Eight-foot-high, two-and-a-half-inch-thick, oak-paneled doors and they wanted them out," he said, shaking his head. Through a scornful *hrummph,* he added, "I saved them." Then he clarified cynically, "The doors, I mean."

Along the north wall, Archie had built massive steel racks to hold his inventory of steel stock. Channel and angle iron, plate steel in various thicknesses, steel rod, round, square, and octagonal stock that ranged in size from one-eighth inch in diameter to six inches in diameter hung from steel posts solidly bolted to the wall. A chain hoist hung from an I beam overhead, ready to lift material into place. In the dark northwest corner of the shop sat an old refrigerator. "I keep my welding rods in there so the air doesn't ruin them," Archie said, as a way of explaining the tarnished, brown-stained old Westinghouse that looked out of place.

As we walked through the large bay, we passed a mechanical hacksaw and a huge vertical boring mill that Archie used to enlarge predrilled holes in thick steel. Sitting next to the mill was a pedestal grinder with a couple of ten-inch grinding wheels, one coarse and one fine, both fully exposed with no guards in place. An old floor stand–model drill press sat next to it.

"Here," Archie commanded, holding a small ball peen hammer, "give it a tap." He was referring to a massive 250-pound anvil that sat proudly on top of a sizable slice from a hard rock maple tree trunk. Sweat from hands, his I assumed, had darkened the lower portion of the heavy hickory handle with a dark brown layer not unlike that found on old, well-used, oil-finished furniture. The balance of the hammer felt good in my hand. It was the first tool I had touched since leaving Pennsylvania, and the feel of it fully awakened my desire to get back to using my hands. I lifted the hammer and lightly tapped the anvil, which responded with a high-pitched ring that lingered in the dusky air of the shop. "That's a great sound, Archie."

"It better be. It cost me a dime to get it!"

"A what?" I asked surprised. "What do you mean, it cost you a dime?"

"You have to get the anvil squared up, Deek, otherwise it won't ring. Here, look." His finger pointed to the edge of a tarnished dime that stuck out of one corner of the anvil where it met the maple. "The ring only means that the hammer will get some bounce when it hits—no sense in wasting energy."

No doubt, Archie was a quirky one, but with each bit of information he threw my way I had another reason to like the man. He led me toward the open door. As I was about to step into the warmth of the spring day, my eyes were drawn once again to the small lathe that sat just to the right of the door. Looking at the lathe, I said to Archie, "If you ever need to have someone to help out with the work, feel free to call on me."

"What do you know about this kind of work? I thought that you were a teacher," Archie demanded, taking on his menacing tone.

"My grandfather was a craftsman. I learned a lot from him," I answered quietly.

Seeing me looking at the lathe, Archie asked, "Ever work on one?"

"Yes, but I don't have anywhere near the experience that you do."

Emphatically, he declared, "I'll tell you right now, don't expect me to teach you anything. I don't give away what I know."

Purposely remaining calm, I responded, "That's okay with me, Archie. I just need to work in a shop again."

"Oh, you do?"

"Yes, I do. I really do," I said earnestly as we stepped out of the shop.

Archie closed, bolted, and locked the door. As we walked slowly back down the gravel driveway that led to his house, I felt as if I were returning to another world.

Seeing us reappear from behind the garage, Lillian, Bonnie, Kim, and Jason walked over to our car. "Did you enjoy the shop?" Lillian smiled.

"Just unbelievable, just like the day."

As Lillian said good-bye to Kim, Jason, and Bonnie, I raised my hand to shake Archie's. "Thanks, Archie, it was good to meet you."

"Good to meet you too, Deek," he said as we shook hands. Dropping his hand, he hesitated, then said, "Now, if you want to do some work, come down to my shop next Saturday morning. I'm sure that I can find something for you to do."

"What time?" I asked enthusiastically.

"Early," responded Archie, then he turned and walked toward the house.

# 2 · Initiation

How to Become a Machinist
1. Keep your cutting tools sharp.
2. Look at your drawing carefully before starting your job.
3. Be sure your machine is set up right before starting to work.
4. Take your measurements accurately.
5. Keep your machine well oiled, clean, and neat. Personal neatness will give you personality.
6. Take an interest in your job; don't feel that you are forced to work.
7. Learn the fundamentals of mechanical drawing.
8. Keep your belts tight and free from oil.
9. Take as heavy a cut as the machine and cutting tool will stand until you are near the finished size; then finish carefully and accurately.

10. *Try to understand the mechanism of the machine you are operating.*
11. *Hold yourself responsible for the job you are working on.*
12. *Keep your eyes on the man ahead of you; you may be called on to take his place some day.*
13. *Have a place for everything and keep everything in its place.*
14. *Read one or two of the technical magazines relating to your line of work.*
15. *If a boy learns a trade properly he becomes a first-class mechanic, but if he has ability he need not stop at that.*
16. *If you have spoiled a job, admit your carelessness to your foreman, and don't offer any excuses.*
17. *Before starting to work on a lathe, roll up your sleeves and remove your necktie—safety pays.*

South Bend Lathe Works, *How to Run a Lathe*, 1952

E arly the next Saturday morning, I raced down to Archie's shop. Peering into the dimly lit void I had visited the Sunday before, my eyes strained to adjust from the bright morning sun, trying to catch a glimpse of Archie. There was only dusky yellow light and silence. I ventured forth, stepping into the cool space to see Archie slowly moving in my direction. Dressed in well-worn blue herringbone coveralls and a dark green cap with an oil-stained visor that glistened as if it were made of polished ebony, the blending of Archie and his machines was even more complete than it had been during my shop tour. This was the first time that I saw Archie donning his work clothes and it was a reminder that, unlike our first meeting, this time it was serious business. "Good morning, Deek, thought you'd never get here, the day's nearly over." It was a few minutes after eight.

"Good morning, Archie."

"Well, are you ready to go to work?"

"What do you have in mind?"

"Oh, just something to get you started on that little lathe you like so much," he said, a smirk spreading across his face. He turned, disappearing into a dark corner of the shop. My guess was that he was going to get some steel stock for cutting and I took the brief moment to gather my wits about myself. Did I really remember how to true a piece of stock in the chuck? What would Archie ask me to machine? To what tolerance? Did he expect me to sharpen my own cutting tools? Doubt entered the picture, the same foreboding that attacked me backstage whenever I was facing an hour or so of solo singing. Such audacity! Who was I to presume that I could walk into another man's shop and offer my services? Working by myself building or restoring, I relied on myself—when I screwed up, I had only myself to blame. I set my own deadlines, procrastinated about making a critical cut, and covered my errors with a remake or design change with impunity. Working with Archie would be a different matter and possibly quite dangerous—a lathe doesn't discriminate between cutting steel or cutting fingers. Torque is torque.

I walked over to the little lathe. Inspired by her purposeful, friendly appearance, my confidence returned, my bout of insecurity transformed to eagerness the same way it always did when I walked out on stage.

Sitting on her strong cast-iron legs, the lathe was ready. The universal chuck waited to receive the steel. The forward/reverse switch sat throne-like with its small lever topped off with a well-rubbed reddish knob. The carriage sat like a piece of kinetic sculpture with gleaming wheels and levers that asked to be touched and moved. The cross slide and compound held a newly sharpened cutting tool. The ways, a cast-iron bed upon which the carriage moved, reflected an oily luster.

Archie reappeared with his arms behind him and shoulders somewhat slouched, the same posture he used when he walked me around his beloved Fords. Walking to where I stood, he looked me square in the eye. "Let me ask you a question. If you know so much about using a lathe, then you must know the parts that move and the parts that don't?"

Whatever guise he thought sheltered his intent, it was not nearly thick enough to hide the fact that he was setting me up. Sure that I could match his wits, I asked, "I'm not sure what you mean."

"It's plain enough, Deek. Do you know the parts that move and the parts that don't? That's all I'm asking."

"I never thought of it that way, but sure I do," I answered, playing along.

"And you're sure that you want to work on this lathe?" he asked, further exercising his authority.

"I'm sure," I replied assuredly, covering my apprehension.

"Then here," he said as his hands came from around his back with a can of green machinery paint in one and a brush in the other. "Paint the parts that don't."

"You want me to paint the lathe?" I asked in protest. "Is that what all these questions are about?"

"Yup," he said calmly. "You said you wanted to work on it, didn't you? Or don't you consider painting work?"

I looked at Archie with half a smile on my face. Archie's move was classic. He had put me in my place and I knew it; in fact, I relished it. Tricking me into painting the lathe was the kind of grab-ass tomfoolery that defined the workshops of my childhood, and I hadn't had a brush with it since before graduate school. As far as I'm concerned, you can't experience this kind of banter anywhere but in a place where men work with their hands. There are key phrases that suggest such teasing is about to begin. Archie's *Let me ask you a question* leads the list, and I was proud that I picked it up, thanks to the shoptalk of my youth. I had a few choices. Either not say a word and go about painting the lathe, walk out never to set foot in the place again, or call upon some early childhood initiations and trust that they were universal in their application. I chose the last and moved to an offensive position.

"This is green paint. Do you want it all one color? How about gray for the gear cover?"

"Yup," Archie responded, playing along, much to my relief, as if we were making an important decision.

"Well, where is it?" I asked, taking on Archie's tone. "I like painting top down. Saves work."

"I thought you said you were a teacher. What do you know about work?" Archie retorted.

"A hell of a lot, but that's not why I'm here. If I'm going to paint the lathe, then I want to use some gray on it."

"You always curse when you're nervous?" Then, mumbling something under his breath, Archie turned away, went back to the corner of the shop, and returned with a can of gray paint. I was triumphant.

"Don't forget to stir the paint, or don't you know anything about painting either?"

"How about some mineral spirits to clean the brush?"

"Use gas. It's in that can over there."

"Gas? Isn't that dangerous?"

"Not half as dangerous as having a teacher around. Use it outside. I've got work to do."

Archie left me standing by the small lathe as he walked down the aisle of machines to his bench. I had passed the first test, otherwise he would have tossed me out of his shop. I felt good about that, even though painting the lathe was not at all what I had in mind. The lathe was clean of oil or dirt and ready for a coat of paint, and I surmised that Archie had anticipated that I would do the painting. Exercising my authority, I decided to paint the gear cover and other *parts that don't move* gray, saving green for the legs.

I suppose that if Archie really wanted to nail me, he would have had me paint some lesser machine, say, the bench grinder. As it was, I was about to paint the heart of a machine shop. There is nothing that we use or drive or fly in or do that isn't in some way or another linked to a metal-cutting lathe. It is at the heart of everything industrial and without a doubt, it is the most important piece of machinery ever conceived by the human mind. And, damn it, Archie's comment notwithstanding, I was going to paint one of them.

The little lathe was a South Bend, nine-inch, floor leg model and, as lathes go, it was a simple enough machine. It was capable of cutting pieces of steel with a swing of no more than nine inches and a maximum length of about twenty inches. By changing the leather belt from pulley to pulley, the operator could adjust the speed of the chuck: slow for heavy cuts, faster for fine cuts and polishing. With a few adjustments to this and that lever, it could machine screws, bore a hole, or cut a disc from a piece of stock. There were a lot of things that a lathe could do, and its few limitations are probably more related to human frailty than to the laws of nature.

I had seen many lathes, but this was the first time I saw what looked like an old automobile transmission sitting between the electric motor and the lathe. "What's this?" I called to Archie, getting his attention.

"What?"

"This," I said, moving the cut-off shift lever.

"It's a transmission and keep your hands and that paint brush away from it. Don't bother me anymore. I'm busy."

As I learned later, the transmission was actually from a Model A, and Archie had rigged it to have more control over the speed settings of the lathe. When it came down to it, there wasn't a machine in his shop that didn't have one or another alterations to better suit Archie's way of working.

I settled into painting. From behind brush and paint, I observed Archie's purposeful movements as he worked at the big lathe. He worked at a steady pace, his movements deliberate. He reached for switches, cranks, and wheels that jutted from the lathe with the alacrity of a pianist performing Liszt. His hands knew where they had put things or exactly where a lever or knob was located—habitual movements that came from years of experience at that machine. Now and then he would stop the lathe, reach for a caliper, and check the measurements of the piece. Then, flicking on the motor, he would go back to spinning ever finer twirls of steel from the turning stock. When he reached a preordained tolerance, he would retract the carriage, loosen the binding lever of the tail stock, retract the center post, open the chuck, and take the warm, finished piece from the lathe to set it gently on the worn top of the wooden bench top behind him—all accomplished in one fluid motion.

Catching my eye while blowing some metal cuttings away from his lathe with a conveniently placed air hose, he said, "Never set the air pressure above forty pounds. Too much air pressure could send one of these pieces of cuttings into your eye or even under your skin." I could have responded to his comment with a sarcastic "no kidding" as any beginning machinist should know this; instead, I nodded my head. His effort to advise me was a minor contradiction to the emphatic comment he had made earlier about his unwillingness to give up any of his knowledge, and I took it as a crack in his armored personality.

Painting was cathartic, even though it is my least favorite activity—I'd rather sling a sledgehammer than paint. Perhaps painting the lathe was penance for leaving my hands idle since leaving Wilkes-Barre and the flooded house. If this was penance, then it surely was a price I was willing to pay if it would lead me back to my other half. My hands had become softened, their palm creases clean and white. The calluses of a working childhood were gone, but not the scars. I took inventory: There was one from a drawknife, another from a jack plane, a nasty one from an errant crosscut saw and a few others that escaped identification. Surely, I could do without any more cuts, but I couldn't do without some calluses, and I was determined to get them.

"You must be done, sitting there looking at your hands," Archie said, quipping. "Pretty colorful," he observed as he came up next to me.

"If you're going to paint a lathe, you might as well do it right, Archie. You know, I've never heard of anyone painting a lathe before. In fact, I felt a little bad covering up her patina. I mean, she had some years of marks on her, you know? She had character."

"*She* had *character*?" What do you mean '*she* had *character*'?"

"From all the hands that used her, that made things, that labored over her, that's what I mean. Don't you think that machines take on character?"

"Nope. And I don't think they become women either," Archie answered in a flat tone

"Well, Archie, I'll call it character."

"I'll tell you what character is, Deek, and it has nothing to do with machines. It's what you make from them that counts. It's either right or it's wrong, plain and simple. Character is doing things right and if you don't know that, you might as well go back to teaching. Now let's get back to work." Providing no time for any response, he thrust out his hand. "Here," he said, handing me about ten short pieces of one-inch flat stock, "how about easing the edges off these pieces? Use the grinder over there."

Damn if he didn't send me to the one machine I could do without. And to make matters worse, it would be the first machine I would use in his shop. A grinder! For chrissake, I thought, is this where this shop business is leading, grinding edges like I did when I was ten.

Without hesitation, I took the pieces of cold steel, but unwilling to yield to his comments about machinery, I said, "I can't agree Archie. I mean if you work at a machine for a long time, it wears into your way of working and to me that's taking on character."

"Oh, Deek, now that's different. Wearing this way or that, a machine is like us. They pick up quirks."

"That's what I mean, Archie. Taking all those quirks together. Isn't that character?"

"Nope, it's called wearing out. See that lathe over there?" he said, pointing to his big lathe. "Why, I've been working so long at that lathe that nobody else could ever get it to do what I get out of it. But that's not character."

"Well, what is it then? What do you call it?" I asked.

"Teacher," he said, "it just is. Why do you want a word for it? It's wearing out, just like you and me and this conversation. That's all there is to it." He pointed to the grinder. "Now, don't grind those pieces to nothing, just ease them."

I headed to an old pedestal grinder with unguarded, exposed, ten-inch diameter, one-inch-thick abrasive wheels on each end. "Put on the glasses," Archie yelled from across the shop. "No sense tearing your eye out." Hanging from the switch that jutted out in front of the grinder was an old pair of safety glasses, which I slipped over my head.

The grinder started with a menacing gnarl, turning the abrasive wheels at a speed of around 2,500 r.p.m. I took each of the pieces and carefully eased their edges as directed, thinking that at any moment a piece of wheel was going to break off and tear through me like a rocket. In a few minutes, the mundane but dangerous chore was completed, and I switched off the motor with a sigh of relief.

"When you get white sparks off of the grinding wheel, the steel is good quality. Red sparks mean cheaper steel," Archie said casually, walking over as the whir of the spinning wheels slowly diminished. His tone becoming sarcastic, he asked, "How did *she* do—enough *character* for you?"

"Oh, yeah, Archie, she has lots of character—dangerous as hell," I answered, relieved to back away from the grinder.

"*She* can give you a start, can't *she?*" Archie jested, pushing through a chuckle. "Well, time for tea."

"What tea, you mean we're taking a break?" I asked.

"Yup, we're going to the Indianhead."

"The what?"

Archie ignored my question as he maneuvered his way out of his coveralls. I went out into the mid-morning, seventy-degree, spring day and took a deep breath. The air was clean and vibrant, the sky a soft, clear blue. I smiled at myself, thinking about painting the lathe and using the grinder. I recognized it for what it was, an initiation into working in his shop. I guessed that Archie was tuned in to how important it was for me to be in his shop, and the thought was entirely gratifying.

Archie came out of the shop, closed, and locked the door and led the way to his three-quarter-ton Chevy pickup truck that was parked next to the three-bay, antique car–filled garages. "Let's go, Deek." I climbed into the cab feeling like I was an eighth grader riding shotgun. The fact that I was a grown man didn't make an ounce of difference.

The Indianhead Cafe stood at the intersection of highways 8 and 27, the east/west and north/south routes that bisected town. Route 8 was the busiest of the two, as it was the connecting highway between upper Michigan and northern Minnesota. Route 27 was used chiefly by people heading north into the wilds of Cheqamegon National Forest and some of the best fishing in North America. Interstates didn't reach this far into the north country, the closest being in Eau Claire, some sixty miles south. For years, the Indianhead Cafe was a popular way station, serving coffee and hearty meals to weary travelers and truck drivers. To the locals, the Indianhead was a place to sit and have a cup of coffee. Or in Archie's case, tea. Archie led me into the cafe, where he was greeted by each man sitting around the outside of a U-shaped counter.

"Hi, Archie."

"What's new there, Archie?"

"Ya been workin', Archie?"

A sturdy waitress whose territory was the inside of the U asked, "The usual, Archie?" Then, looking at me, she asked flatly, "What can I get for you?" I ordered coffee, which I promptly received accompanied by the noisy clang of its overweight cup hitting the counter. Archie doctored his tea with two teaspoons of sugar and milk, enough to turn the liquid to an off-white color. He made no conversation with me or anyone. In fact, no one sitting at the counter said a word. Each of the men wore caps, including Archie. With the exception of the waitress, who wore a red plastic band around her head, I was the only bareheaded person there, and Archie was the only patron with a hat clear of a medallion advertising everything from Mobil Oil to Agway Feed. I was relieved when, after ten minutes or so, Archie nudged me, stood up, and made for the door.

On the way back to the shop, Archie asked, "Well, Deek, what do you think of the Indianhead. Quite a place, isn't it?"

"Strange," I answered truthfully. "Everyone said hello, then silence. No one spoke the whole time we sat there. I think it's a strange place, that's what I think." I added, " Did I thank you for the coffee?"

"Yup, you did and no, it's not so strange, Deek. What would be strange is if those boys said anything that was worth hearing. Better to have quiet than hear them talking nonsense."

"Why do you go there, Archie?" I asked.

"For a cup of tea. I've been doing it for years. Keeps my feet to the ground. That's enough questions from the teacher."

With that we drove the mile or so to his shop, got out of his truck, and went back to the shop. Dressed once again in his blue coveralls, Archie said, "Come over here, Deek, let's get this thing up on the bench." I had no idea what the thing was, but it was heavy and very awkward to move from its place on the floor up onto the round heavy steel welding table that sat next to the anvil.

"What is this, Archie?"

"It's a part I'm building for a fellow up in Prentice."

Once the piece was clamped to the bench, I asked, "Where's Prentice?"

"East of town. Here," Archie said, handing me a stout C-clamp, "clamp that piece of angle iron on the edge so it's just touching the line. Ever weld before?"

"Yes, some, mostly with acetylene though."

"Ever weld with an electric arc?" Archie asked again.

"Forge welded, with my grandfather a few times, and yes, I've used an arc welder." Obviously, I was still in a defensive mode.

By the time I answered, Archie had attached a heavy, insulated lead from his arc welder, an old beast of a machine, to the piece of steel. "Better get a helmet if you're going to watch this," he said, as he put an eighth-inch welding rod into the electrode holder located at the end of another lead coming from the welder. As instructed, I put on a welding helmet and, looking through the dark glass, watched Archie weld the angle iron in place, laying an even bead of molten steel at the ninety-degree intersection of the two pieces. I felt the heat strike my body. My eyes caught bright blue flashes that were bouncing off of the wall and sneaking around the sides of the ill-fitting helmet. Stopping for a moment and raising his helmet, Archie handed me a chipping hammer and commanded, "Clean up the weld."

I tapped the new weld to loosen the glassy residue left by the flux of the rod, a job that I had done many times in my youth. Still in the initiation stages, I thought. "You want to give it a try?" he said, after I gave the weld a few final taps with the chipping hammer.

I took the hefty, well-worn electrode holder in my now gloved right hand and brought the rod to the steel, where it stuck fast, causing a deep-throated hum of indignation to come from the old welder. I wiggled the rod to break it from its hold, which it did with the hissing, crackling blue arc of a hundred amps.

"A little early to celebrate the fourth," Archie said, laughing. "Just stroke it lightly, Deek, go easy. Let yourself flow with the weld."

A few more stokes and the melting steel flowed easily. My arm and hand relaxed as the tiny mounds of steel lay down in neat, patterned, overlapping arcs, not unlike the scales of a fish. "Now you've got it, Deek, good work," I heard Archie say through the spitting sounds of joining steel.

When the weld was complete, I chipped off the hard, brittle residue, looked at Archie, and said, "Thanks for the lesson."

"I'm no teacher, Deek," Archie retorted. "You're the one that did the weld, not me. Now let it sit and cool," he said, referring to the steel.

His comment *Let yourself flow with the weld,* dug as deep into my mind as the weld had in the steel—it was personal as opposed to technical, more artistic than practical. With his lesson on Jo blocks and his comments pertaining to red and white sparks and not going above 40 psi when blowing shards of metal off of a machine and now advice that was encouraging and personal, I felt a familial tug.

The idea that he and I were becoming linked in a surrogate father-son relationship crossed my mind. The death of my father and having left a grandfather a thousand miles back east left me vulnerable, and it would have been easy for me to assign either role to Archie. Further, Lillian had told Bonnie that she and Archie had no children and, from that, I surmised that Archie, at age seventy, was as vulnerable as I was. The issue was further complicated by my young children, Kim and Jason, who would most certainly benefit by having Archie fill the role of Grandpa.

But I wanted friendship, not fathering. I needed to be in the presence of an older man, a craftsman, who could provide the balance between my intellectual life of college teaching and my need to work with my hands. I had weathered the longest, coldest winter I could ever have imagined with only the intellectual and social spin-offs of teaching at a college, and it nearly killed me. I saw Archie as the person who would add balance to my life and I was convinced that wouldn't happen if he and I fell into father-son roles.

With work completed, we cleaned up our mess, swept the floor, and made sure that everything was in its place. It was noon and, being Saturday, time to quit. Once again, Archie slid out of his coveralls. Looking at my filthy dungarees and red flannel shirt, he said, "You're pretty dirty, Deek. Maybe you ought to get some of these." He hung his limp, baggy coveralls on a nail behind the door.

"No," I responded with more certainty than was needed, "I prefer dungarees and a shirt." I regretted using such a heavy hand, which was more connected to my thoughts of replacing my father and grandfather than it was with practicality.

"No need to get upset. I'll bet if you did your own wash, you'd think differently. But besides that, if you're going to work in my shop, you'll wear the right clothes, and as far as I'm concerned that doesn't include your Sunday-go-meetin' outfit," Archie said seriously.

"You're right Archie, sorry. I'll get a pair this week."

We washed our hands using a white, Crisco-like mixture that said WITH LANOLINE in red letters on its can, then rinsed them in a wooden barrel of murky water. In leaving the shop, I thanked Archie for a good day. "How about next Saturday?" he asked.

"What time?"

"Early," Archie said, then turned away and walked down the gravel driveway.

I made the mile drive home thinking about the day: I painted a lathe gray and green, ground off some rough edges on pieces of flat steel, had a cup of coffee at the silent counter of the local beanery, and helped Archie weld some steel. The cuticles of my fingers were outlined in black, and even though Archie's hand soap claimed to "leave your hands soft and clean," embedded in my palms was black oily dirt from handling steel stock. A streak of gray paint was on the back side of my right hand. The morning had been well spent. My visit confirmed what I suspected when I first met Archie only a week earlier: He was a master craftsman, intelligent, witty, and potentially, a good friend. I was confused over his constant reference to my being a teacher and it troubled me but I was determined not to let it interfere with what I felt was a growing friendship. The Welsh word *hiraeth* came to mind. Not easily translated, it means feeling right in a geographical sense. That's what I felt when I was in Archie's shop. It was the right place to be. *Hiraeth*.

# 3 · The Little Lathe

*The screw cutting engine lathe is the oldest and most important of machine tools and from it all other machine tools have been developed. It was the lathe that made possible the building of the steamboat, the locomotive, the electric motor, the automobile and all kinds of machinery used in industry. Without the lathe our great industrial progress of the last century would have been impossible.*

South Bend Lathe Works, *How to Run a Lathe*, 1952

Archie handed me a twelve-inch bar of one-inch diameter cold rolled steel stock. "Here, Deek, turn this down to thirteen sixteenths."

"How long?"

"Go nine inches, it's going to be a shaft for this gear housing," he offered. "I'll adjust it later."

"I assume you want me to turn it down on the small lathe," I asked, not hiding my enthusiasm.

"Well, where else? You're sure not going to the grinder with it. Anyway, *she* sat so pretty waiting for you, I just couldn't take it anymore," he teased, taking on a singsong voice that was foreign to Archie's character. It was almost as alien as me wearing herringbone coveralls, which I was doing this morning. Noticing my discomfort, Archie added, "Anyway, you look so new in those clothes that, well, I thought you and lathe would make a good couple."

I had taken Archie's advice and bought a pair of coveralls through the Wards catalog store. To be honest, I was pretty eager to get them. The clerk, who knew me as a college teacher, asked, "Why do you need these, something special going on at the college?"

"No, but I need them for Saturday morning." She promised that my Monday order would arrive by week's end. I kept my working with Archie to myself and told the clerk that I had things to do, which seemed to satisfy her. I must admit, when I tried on the coveralls, I felt good about it, as if I were donning the costume of a working man instead of the customary suit and tie that came with teaching. I was a bit uncomfortable that the long sleeves of the coveralls might present a hazard while working around the uncaring twirl of machinery, a warning I had received from Grandpa, but I decided I would roll them up or cut them off if needed. The package from Wards arrived on Thursday, and the first thing I did was wash them, hoping to relieve some of the newness that would surely be a target of Archie's ridicule. Even wearing them to do some dirty garage work at home, however, didn't seem to make a difference. It would be a while before they were broken in enough to not look conspicuous in the shop.

The South Bend that I had painted a week ago was as clean as I had left it and other than a freshly sharpened cutting tool sitting proud in its tool post, I doubted that Archie had used her during the week. *Her*, I thought. I didn't know why I ascribed the feminine gender to machines, nor throughout a busy week of preparing my students for finals did this question pop into my mind much.

In every shop that I visited as a child, the machines were referred to as *she*. I clearly recalled a time visiting one of my grandfather's shops in Mauch Chunk (a town that has since changed its name to Jim Thorpe in honor of the great Indian athlete that came from there), watching nineteen- and twenty-year-old men learning their craft on row upon row of all kinds of machine tools. During a break from their projects, I overheard one of them saying, "She's working beautifully today."

Another commented, "Mine isn't, she's putting up quite a fight."

They were talking about the lathes on which they were working. Another fellow piped in, taking the banter a bit further. "Well mine's working pretty good, a little better than she did last night. Hell, she nearly broke my back with all her twisting and turning."

Grandpa's boys were getting a bit randy and he moved right in to water them down, as he was fond of saying. "You boys show more respect around here. Anyway"—referring to me—"there's a young boy here. Now, what's this business about she this and she that?" he asked, demanding that his "boys" own up.

"We're referring to the machines, sir," a fellow piped in obviously bent on getting his peers off the hook. "Machines can't be pushed, that's all," he said, with deep conviction. In a deeper, even more reverent tone, he continued, "They all have different qualities, wants, and needs. You have to get to know them, work with them, be kind to them. If you do that, they will work with you all day without any trouble." The other young men hastily nodded in agreement.

"Get back to work," Grandpa commanded, shaking his head as he walked away.

That was 1952. And as far as I was concerned, Grandpa didn't have to worry about protecting my ten-year-old innocence. His "boys" made sure I was up on the boy-girl stuff, and while I didn't understand all of it, I knew pretty much what was going on.

Here I was twenty-two years later in Archie's shop and, with the exception of understanding a lot more about boy-girl stuff, not much had changed. I still heartily agreed with Grandpa's boys: Machines are feminine, at least as far as I was concerned. Archie's opposing view notwithstanding, my little lathe (I assumed ownership) was a *she*, and *we* were a couple. I got down to work.

I set the bar of rough steel stock on a well-worn wooden tray attached under the lathe and proceeded to get her set up. Shaving three sixteenths of an inch off of the bar would take a seasoned machinist a few moments, but after about fourteen years away from using a lathe, I needed to move more slowly.

Using a heavy chuck key, I opened the universal chuck, which operates much like the chuck in a hand drill, reached down to the shelf to retrieve the steel bar, and slid it into the chuck until about three inches protruded. Next, I simultaneously tightened the three jaws securely around the steel bar and set the cutting tool to dead center of the face of the shaft, slightly backing off the compound rest to give clearance between the cutter and the work. Reaching up with my left hand, I felt the small red knob of the switch lever, turned it to the right, and the lathe leapt to life with a speed that set a high whine spinning about the shop. Instantly, I reached for the switch and turned off the power.

"Too fast, Deek. Too fast. What are you trying to do, launch the thing?" Archie yelled out from across the shop, where he was cutting lengths of steel rod at the mechanical hacksaw.

By the time the lathe ceased motion, Archie was by my side.

"Deek, you forgot to check the speed," Archie said as he reached for a lever that sat between the lathe and its rear-mounted motor. Loosening the tension of the wide leather belt, Archie slid the belt along the conical pulleys until he was satisfied. Then he reached for a lever that stuck out of the modified Model A transmission.

"When you painted the lathe you moved the lever; otherwise, things would have been all right," Archie admonished. Shifting the transmission, he said, "There, now, you don't need to go any faster than where it is. Now, I'm only going to say this once. Never, never start a machine without knowing exactly what it's going to do. If you're ever surprised by a machine, it means you're out of control, and that can get you killed."

I felt a bit foolish but knew that I deserved the lecture. Too much romance with the lathe, I reasoned, got me into trouble. I was lucky I still had my body intact.

"By the way, Deek," Archie's tone changed to a shy, singsong lilt, "don't fool around with things that might get you in trouble. Especially with *her*. Why, *she* just might get away from you again, you never know where *she* might run to." He laughed in his squeaky voice as he returned down the aisle.

I didn't say a word because there were no words to say. Instead, I took a deep breath and began anew.

Once I was sure that everything was in order, I flipped the switch lever to the right. A deep yawn came from the motor as it quickly got up to speed. With its smooth, well-lubricated, spinning bearings singing merrily to the hefty rhyme of the slapping leather belt, the cooperative and yearning hum of the little lathe resonated throughout the shop. This is the sound I yearned to hear, a deep, rich sound that I felt as much as I heard, connecting me to the work by some magic, invisible cord. There is no sound to equal it, although I'm sure that my father would have found a singer who came close—probably John Charles Thomas. For him, it wasn't machines that produced magical sounds, but humans. Dad would associate singers with sounds of everyday life. If he liked a singer, he or she was likened to the power of, say, a steam locomotive or the sweetness of a robin. When he heard a singer he didn't like, he described the poor soul using words like rasp, cough, fart, disgusting. Dad was very descriptive when it came to singers. This motor's sound, however, would never have come close to stirring him the way it stirred me now.

Turning a satiny wheel that sat at hip's height, I slowly brought the carriage close to the spinning steel until the sharpened tip of the cutting tool bit purposefully into the face of the turning bar. Responsively, my hand moved from the carriage wheel to a small crank that controlled the cross slide. Turning it in a counterclockwise direction to bring the cutting tool gracefully along the face of the turning stock, a spiral of thin steel spun from the tip of the cutting tool, exposing the shiny, fresh interior of the raw steel. When the cutting tool was past the diameter of the stock, I reached down to the wheel that controlled the carriage and, turning it clockwise, withdrew the cutting tool from the now smooth-faced end of the stock. I reached up and switched off the motor.

"Well, how's it going over there?" Archie asked, his voice coming from across the shop.

"Just fine, Archie, just fine."

"Are you done with that piece yet?" he jostled. "Is *she* being good to you?"

"Just getting started, Archie," I answered with impatience. Archie's choice of words, however witty his attempt, was grating on my nerves.

"Just asking, Deek, just asking."

Taking the bar of steel out of the chuck, I turned it around and repeated the process on the other end. Then, placing a centering bit in the tailstock and moving it almost against the smooth face of the bar, I switched on the lathe and drilled a small, countersunk hole in its center. Turning off the motor, I withdrew the tailstock, loosened the chuck, pulled out about ten inches and retightened the jaws. Replacing the centering bit and toolstock chuck with a dead center, I slid the tailstock in place and tightened it to the bed. Putting a few drops of white lead in the countersunk hole at the end of the stock, I turned the tailstock crank until the center rested firmly in the hole. Held fast in place, the stock was ready for machining. With the tip of the cutting tool slightly above center and perpendicular to the stock, I made a few passes along the bar. The pungent aroma of hot steel that mixed with the vapor left from the cutting oil reached my nose, bringing with it the peace of good childhood memories.

The years that had separated my adolescent hands from when they last worked at a lathe dissipated like melting ice. My body remembered the geography of it all, the forward/reverse switch, the movement of the carriage and the tailstock, the glorious sound of perfectly balanced spinning steel. I smiled to myself, nodding my head as if to remind my brain that its body is no fool, thank you very much. The calipers indicated thirteen six-teenths of an inch—dead on. Crunching underfoot were bits of oily steel.

The warmth and sheen of the newly turned work brought life to what was only a bar of cold steel a half hour earlier—creating a new reality, as James Joyce said about the meaning of art. Withdrawing the stock from the chuck, I carefully wiped off the cutting oil before bringing it to Archie.

"Here it is, Archie. What do you think?"

"It looks okay to me. Can you cut it off at eight inches? And ease the ends, they're a bit sharp," he said in clipped, punitive tones.

"Why didn't you tell me that earlier?" I protested. "Now I have to set up again."

"I thought you knew what to do. You're the teacher, not me," he responded underhandedly.

Unlike the grab-ass tomfoolery that circulated around my ascribing gender to machines, in this case, Archie's initial direc-tion to cut the bar at nine inches, then send me back to cut it down to eight inches was, in shop parlance, bullshit. Restraining myself, I asked in a plain tone, "Archie, what does my being a teacher have to do with you giving me the wrong directions? You wanted nine inches, I gave you nine inches."

Ignoring my question about his reference to my being a teacher, he said in an unruffled tone, "Well now I want eight. Use the hacksaw. I'd like to get done sometime today."

"Me too," I said. Rather than push the issue, I headed for the hacksaw, where in less than a minute I cut the piece to the desired length.

Returning to the lathe from the hacksaw, I finished the end and, using a file, softened its edge. "Before I take this thing out of the lathe, do you have any more surprises?" I asked.

"Nope, but leave it there, it's time for tea."

Like the week before, we drove in Archie's truck to the Indianhead for what was becoming a Saturday morning ritual. The same group of tired-looking men sat around the counter with their heads bowed, looking, I presumed, into their cups. It was a dismal scene. As we went into the cafe, the men raised their heads, made salutations to Archie, then fell silent. Without asking, the waitress noisily put a cup of coffee in front of me after delivering Archie's tea. By the time I finished the coffee, it was cold, as the heavy cup absorbed every therm it could get. A poster announcing the college chorus's spring concert was prominently displayed on the wall opposite where Archie and I were sitting. I said nothing, hoping that he would notice, but he remained silent.

On our way back to the shop, I asked him if he had seen the poster.

"Nope," he responded.

"It was announcing our upcoming chorus concert. You want tickets? On me," I declared.

"Nope."

I didn't push him. His response was final and said with the tone one might get from hitting a block of lead with a sledgehammer.

"Well, Deek, let's finish up," Archie said as we pulled into the driveway. "A few more cuts will do."

"A few more cuts?" I asked warily.

"Yup, but this time I'm moving you over to the miller. Do you know how to use one?"

A milling machine, which is second in importance to a lathe in a machine shop, is used for a variety of applications, most of which are associated with surfacing or planing steel.

"It's been a long time, Archie, but I'll give it a whirl."

"Keep your whirling for the lathe, Deek," Archie quipped. "I just want you to cut a keyway, and this time, I'll be right next to you to be sure you don't turn on the switch until you turn on your head."

Archie assigned me the task of cutting a Woodruff key slot in a place he marked on the shaft I had finished earlier. Shaped like a half moon, a Woodruff key is a flat piece of steel available in varying sizes and is used to prevent a wheel or gear from spinning on a shaft. In this case, the key was to slide into a corresponding groove cut into the inside diameter of one of the gears that Archie had made. Using a milling machine with a small-toothed cutting wheel would do the job in a jiffy. Archie guided me through setting up the miller and in about twenty minutes from setup to cleanup, I had the keyway cut.

As occurred when I ran the lathe earlier in the morning, the sounds and oily smell of the miller awakened some childhood memories stored away for just such an occasion, only in this case, my remembering was not silent.

Archie's miller was a bit taller than I am, probably about seventy-five inches or so. In contrast to the lathe, which lay horizontal, and, even though heavily built, gave the impression of lightness, the miller was vertical and very heavy in appearance—my guess is that it weighed twice as much as the lathe.

(Operatically speaking, if the lathe were Mimi, the miller would be Brunhilda.) As I turned the crank to bring the bed up to the cutting wheel, I heard myself make an explosive sound.

"What was that? Did you say something?" Archie asked from his bench.

"No, Archie, just adjusting things," I said as I buried myself in the work. Archie had heard an explosion, all right, one that came from my mouth when my mind whisked me back into my youth, when Grandpa's miller was the control room of a submarine. It was the explosion a torpedo makes hitting a German U-boat amidships. I smiled at myself—nostalgia is such a trickster.

After polishing the shaft, Archie slid it into a gear housing, inserted the Woodruff key, put the gears he had made in place, then screwed on a gasket-covered cap. The job was done when Archie set the finished product on the floor to the right of the shop door, a place anyone first looked when he came to Archie's shop to pick up completed work. "Time to go, Deek," Archie said, routinely peeling off his seasoned coveralls. "No sense taking those fancy duds home. Here, hang them on the hook behind the door," Archie offered.

After twisting and writhing to get my shoulders free from the grasp of my still stiff coveralls, I hung them next to Archie's. Washing and rinsing off our hands in the murky water of the half wooden barrel provided a soft, relaxing transition from hands-on work to other activities.

As I drove home from Archie's shop, I remembered Grandpa telling me once that a workshop is a sacred place. "By looking at a person's shop," he said, "you peer into his soul." Certainly, I felt that way about Archie's shop, with its shelves of mysterious boxes, old modified machines, and dull incandescent light. But as important as what I saw was what I felt. On the few occasions that I was briefly left alone in his shop, I sensed the same majesty I did when standing on a darkened stage. It was that sense of spirituality that alerted me to the importance of the place.

Reflecting on the day's turn of events, I realized that my move from one machine to another was as carefully worked out by Archie as it was with most of what the man did. My sizing-up time was past. I had entered a new level where trust was beginning to outdistance skepticism, and if I kept at it, a friendship with Archie was ensured.

My work with him reawakened a desire to have my own shop, and it was time I got on with it. I thought of my precious woodworking tools, which, hurriedly packed, still lay in their cartons stored in the basement. I heard myself say out loud the word "tools." I turned the word over in my mouth, feeling its soft *t* melding into a clean *oo*, and finished with a lingering *el* topped off with a cool *z*, pronounced, perhaps, as Ella Fitzgerald would with the word jazz. Just as I did when I spontaneously sang out as a child, I let go with the word "tools" on a high note, spinning it out like a triumphant cry. Too much time had gone by without feeling the energy of those crafting instruments. I now knew it was time to make things whole again and leave behind all the dark days of my first Wisconsin winter. This funk hadn't affected my music making, that's for sure. People living in the small town of Ladysmith and its vast rural environs had enough talent and desire to sing to keep my days and nights packed with rehearsals and concerts. My students received my undivided attention and my family enjoyed new friendships made through school, day care, the college, and church. But I had dismissed my crafts; I couldn't really say why. Perhaps it was post-flood depression or cabin fever, or maybe guilt about leaving my hometown. Whatever it was, it was over. I headed for the basement to unpack my tools, some of which had been with me since childhood.

Without exception, every tool in my collection had a story to tell. I pulled out the rivet hammer that I made in eighth grade shop class out of a square stock of steel using a hacksaw and files to fashion its shape. The sixteen-ounce hammer and twelve-inch hacksaw had the residue of powder blue paint marks on their handles, which I put there at age nine to identify them as mine. I unpacked a nail set that I bought from Wagner Brothers Hardware for ten cents in 1954, the first tool that I ever bought for myself. There was the wood chisel that left a nasty scar at the base of the thumb of my left hand when I tried to force her against the grain. At the bottom of the wooden box where I had packed my special tools, I came across the carefully wrapped wire strippers that Bonnie had given me on Christmas 1967, and the jack plane that Grandpa gave me after one productive Saturday morning in his shop. I found a marking gauge that I had *borrowed* from eight grade shop class.

The last box that I unpacked contained an assortment of screws, bolts, nuts, springs, washers, small pieces of metal, and a number of unidentifiable objects left over from this or that, all mixed together with no rhyme or reason. It was my junk box, and I happily welcomed it to my new shop. There were pieces in my junk box that went back a good ten years, and I could pretty much remember precisely where each nut, bolt, or scrap came from. I would never be without a junk box.

Repairing flood damage had been very tough on my chisels, saws, and planes as fine, gritty silt found its way into even the pores of wood. They became dull, their keen edges, which I used to keep so sharp that they cut light, were reduced to a dusky luster. My tools had taken a beating and so had I, only my tools couldn't right themselves.

Unpacked and cleaned, I began the rewarding chore of sharpening chisels and ending with the plane cutters from my two wood planes. I worked on them until they could cut the hair off my arm; then I knew they were sharp enough. Finished with sharpening, I tuned each tool, taking special care with the planes. A plane is nothing more than a chisel held at a constant angle and it is a relatively uncomplicated tool, but woe be it should a plane be out of adjustment. Instead of smoothing or squaring up a piece of wood, it will mar and tear up a piece in a flash.

To test the tune of my tools, I ran the chisels bevel side up along the edge of a pine board. Much to my satisfaction, thin curls of pine resulted, which I set aside for my daughter Kim to use as decorations for her make-believe cakes. Using the planes, I cut wider curls, practicing until they were so thin that I could make out images when I looked through them. The smell of sweet pine filled my shop and pleasantly stirred my memory.

# 4 · Cherry Wood

*Whether practiced as a trade, an avocation, or simply as a practical adjunct to daily existence, working wood with hand tools satisfies some elemental needs of the human animal—for manual work, development of innate skills, peace and quiet, and a sense of control over his temporal affairs. Listen to the sound of a sharp plane peeling tightly curled shavings from the edge of a board. Sniff the aroma of released oils by which oak and pine are instantly recognizable. Watch the color changes as the surface skin is cut away to underlying layers. Satisfy the sense of touch by brushing the hand over a tool-worked surface, which with experience may become a reliable test of its flatness. And enjoy the feeling of independence when you sit down for a meal at the table you have built with your own hands.*

Aldren A. Watson, Preface, *Hand Tools*, 1982

Ladysmith is a town of 3,800 people located 35 miles north of the forty-fifth parallel and about 125 miles east of Minneapolis. Settled in the late 1800s by lumbermen, the town struggled for its identity, going through four names before the unusual name of Ladysmith was settled on. It was originally called Flambeau Falls, but that hadn't worked because there were no falls, only some roiling rapids. So Falls was dropped, leaving Flambeau. However, there were other locations nearby with the same name, confusing travelers and postmen. So in 1886, the town was named Corbett, in honor of Robert Corbett, the postmaster who perhaps was fed up with all the complaints he'd had about misplaced mail. Two years later, the name of the town changed again. Thinking that the town would attract investors if it carried the name of a prominent businessman, the savvy politicians renamed the town of now one hundred residents Warner, in honor of a powerful figure with the Soo Line Railroad. It didn't work out—I guess that Warner wasn't willing to put his money where his name was. Finally, in 1900, the name Ladysmith was adopted to honor the bride of the president of Menasha Wooden Ware Company, Charles Smith. As the story goes, hopes that the renaming would bring the new couple and their influence to town were dashed when Mrs. Smith refused to move to what she considered a wilderness community. But this time the name stuck.

Ladysmith is a small town surrounded by even smaller towns, making it, relatively speaking, a big town. It is the seat of Rusk County, and today the town is a delightful, energetic community.

Archie was born in Waupaca, Wisconsin, in 1905. When he was five years old, Archie's family moved to Port Arthur, one of the smaller towns surrounding Ladysmith, where his father had purchased a small farm. But as he grew it became apparent that Archie wasn't cut out for planting or milking, so to make up for the time he didn't spend farming, he fixed things. Archie's skills for "fixin' anything he took his fingers to," as his sister Rose once told me, soon led him to Ladysmith, which at the turn of the century was a booming lumber town. Soon Archie was going from wood mill to wood mill sharpening knives and circular saw blades with diameters reaching ten feet and more. Lumbermen sought him out too, because a correctly sharpened blade cut quicker, meaning they made more money with less work. By the time he was sixteen years old, Archie's skills were in demand and had grown to include machining, welding, riveting, and auto mechanics. His reputation for doing good work was soon matched by his reputation for such hell-raising as boxing, bear wrestling, and helping to keep the stills of the north country cooking during Prohibition.

By the time I got to know Archie, his exploits as a young man had reached legendary status, and there were few people in town who didn't have an Archie story or two to tell anyone within earshot. It was hard for me to determine where truth ended and myth began in the stories I heard, but from what I had seen of Archie in his shop, I leaned toward seventy-five percent truth, twenty-five percent tall tale. I wasn't sure, for instance, that I believed the story of his building a still that floated on a swamp that could be sunk when the feds came and raised when they went, but I sure wanted to. But there was no doubt about his reputation for treating people roughly. From what I saw of him, there was no question that his reputation in this respect was right on target.

Even though I only worked with Archie on Saturday mornings, I had some opportunity to observe how gingerly people treated him when they brought things in to be repaired. Those who knew him and his ways deferred to Archie and never made any suggestion about how to repair something. They simply brought him their problem and asked Archie for his help. The more complex the problem, the more Archie welcomed the work. The statement "Archie, I think this is impossible, I just don't see how to make this thing work" brought light into Archie's eyes, and his arms would reach out to embrace the object as if it were a child in need. People who underestimated Archie's ability by asking him to do, as he would say, "something any half-assed fool could do," insulted his ego. When someone did bring something that was easy to repair, Archie would either shake his head no, and send the person to someone else, or depending on his mood, say "leave it here and come back," not specifying a time. The moment the person left the shop, he would take a few minutes to fix it, then set it aside, where it sat out of sight. He always charged more for things that were easy to fix, if in fact he took the time to fix them at all.

Characteristic of many of the machinists that I knew growing up, Archie was most offended by a person who brought him work and made suggestions on how to fix or make it. I had just arrived at Archie's shop one morning when a fellow came in with a broken winch gear. He had received a replacement part, but since he couldn't get it to fit, he came to Archie.

The gear, called a worm ring, was fashioned out of bronze and was made slightly small so that when heated to the proper temperature, it expanded to fit over a corresponding steel hub. When it cooled, it shrank, hugging the steel like bark to a tree. Not knowing this, the man came to Archie asking whether he should cut down the steel hub or enlarge the diameter of the bronze worm ring "so's I could press 'em tight," he said. "Darn company sent me the wrong part and I want to get on with it."

"Do what you want," Archie said coldly. "Why don't you call the company for advice? There's no sense coming to me if you already know how to fix it."

"But, Archie," he protested, "I need the part now. Why don't you just take a few minutes to do some cuts. Hell, it's not that hard a thing to do."

I expected Archie to throw the man out of his shop, but instead Archie took on an authoritative, yet compliant tone of voice, like that, perhaps, of the wolf in "Little Red Riding Hood." "Well, you have a choice. You can leave the thing here and I'll fix it, or you can take it and fix it however you want to fix it."

After a pause, the man said, "I guess I'll leave it here."

"Come back in a few weeks," Archie commanded.

"A few weeks!" the man declared.

"And bring cash," Archie said, now enjoying his position.

The man stood as if he were a student being sent to detention. "I guess I'll come back, Archie," the now contrite man said as he left the shop.

"Here, Deek," Archie said, handing me the parts, "put these things together. The torch is under the metal bench." In less than a half hour the part was cooling and near ready to go. Archie picked it up with a pair of tongs and set it to the right of the shop door, well hidden behind other objects awaiting eager customers.

Archie and I had become friends to a point where fixing something like the worm ring was turned over to me without a comment or care, but I had yet to approach Archie about using any of his machinery to work on projects that I wanted to do. Early on, I was content to simply enjoy working at whatever he had in mind. But now that I had my own woodshop going, I found a number of small things that needed attention. "If it's all the same to you," I said one morning, "I would like to work on this part from a lawn mower I'm putting together. Is there anything else you need me to do?"

Without looking up, Archie said, "I don't know why you're fooling with a lawn mower and I don't want to know. Go ahead, just keep me out of it."

It was not yet nine o'clock when I began working at the lathe and nothing was going right. Seeing my frustration, Archie came over.

"What's wrong?" he inquired.

"Whatever I do with this piece, it's not going to come out right," I said, frustrated over a bad beginning.

"Then it's just plain crazy to keep doing something that isn't ever going to be right," Archie lectured. "Might as well start clean and be done with it. If you can't trust your own feelings, then whose are you going to trust? Now, unless you're in real need for that part in the next few days, just walk away from it and get back to it later. In fact, if you want, I'll fix it for you when I get a chance. Well, you got me into it, didn't you?"

"It wasn't my intention, but, sure, that would be fine with me."

As much as I enjoyed working with steel, my real passion was woodworking. For some time, I had been wanting to tell Archie about my need to get back into my woodshop, but feeling that my confession might interfere with our growing friendship, I hesitated. Standing looking at the lathe holding my ill-begotten piece of work, I felt that the time was right.

"Archie, there's something I need to tell you. As much as I like working with machine tools, my real love is working with wood. Now I don't mean that working here isn't—"

Archie cut me off. "What kind of things do you make?" he asked inquisitively as he stepped back from the lathe.

"Furniture," I told Archie.

I told Archie how, as a child, I loved the feel and look of the dining room furniture that my grandfather made and explained that nine years earlier, I made a cabinet that I gave to Bonnie as a second wedding anniversary gift. I promised at the time that the cabinet was the first piece of a dining room set that I planned to build as the years went by. I revealed to Archie the horrors of the flood and how in the basement of our restored home I had stacked one hundred board feet of cherry that I had planned to use to continue my project. Ending my tale, I said, "When we moved to Ladysmith, I left the cherry behind."

"Cherry is not easy to come by up here. Can't you go back and get your wood?" Archie asked.

Irritated by the thoughts of the flood running through my mind I answered, "Hell no, Archie. Besides, the dumb bastards that bought our house demanded we pay fifty dollars to have the wood hauled away."

"I guess all you need is some cherry—I don't know what you're cursing about. How much do you need?" he asked plainly, with no mention of the flood or its aftermath.

"Well, Archie, I've been giving it some thought and decided to build a china closet before tackling a table and chairs. I guess twenty-five or thirty feet would do," I answered, referring to board feet.

"You're going to need some good grade cherry for that project. Let's lock up the shop and take a look."

Curious, I was about to ask Archie where we were going to look, when Bill Pfalzgraf, Kim's school bus driver, arrived.

"Well, Bill, what's up," Archie said warmly.

"It's the darn bus, Archie. The kingpin's acting up again, and I wonder if you could help me out."

"Bring it in," Archie responded. Turning to me, he said, "You're going to have to wait for that wood, Deek."

The three of us headed back into Archie's shop, where during the next hour, Archie rebuilt the part for the bus. Staying out of Archie's way, I learned from Bill that in addition to driving a school bus, he worked a 150-acre dairy farm. With driving and farming, Bill's day went "From four in the morning until eight o'clock at night. That is, you know, there are shorter days. But, it's not like working in a factory, that's for sure."

"You know," Bill told me, "whenever I come to Archie for help, why, no matter what he's doing, he always stops to lend me a hand. It doesn't matter what I need. If I'm stuck, why, Archie helps me out. He does for all the farmers. Darn good to have a man like Archie ready to help."

"Here's your part, Bill," Archie said, interrupting our casual conversation. "It's better than the original, so you can be sure those kids will have a safe ride."

"How much do I owe you, Archie?"

"Fifteen dollars will do."

Bill opened his wallet, handed over three five dollar bills, then thanked Archie with words and a pat on his left shoulder.

Leaving our coveralls on, Archie locked up, clasped his hands behind his back in his usual pose, and led me down the now familiar gravel driveway and around to the front of the garage by his house. He opened the garage door and I followed him to the rear, where there was a large sliding door that approximated the size of the garage door. Releasing a wooden catch, he slid the door open on its hefty cast-iron wheels, revealing something wonderful. Sawdust! The wonderful, strong, friendly smell of cut wood rolled out of the shop, enveloping me with eau de resin. Archie flicked on bright lights and I stepped inside to a fully equipped woodshop: stacks of wood, machines, laden shelves, and walls covered with tools of all shapes and sizes.

"Where did you get all this, Archie?" I asked in amazement, overwhelmed not only by what I beheld but what I felt—good wood lures me to it like a bear to honey.

"Most of it came from sawmills and woodshops that closed or moved on. Nobody seemed to want the stuff, especially the machinery, but I fixed it up and here it is. Most of it's three-phase, you know, and most places don't have that much current coming in."

I took a moment to look around. There was plenty of light streaming in through three large windows and unlike the lighting in the shop, it was bright, even cheery. His well-used and cared-for workbench sat in the middle of the shop, where it was surrounded by a legion of machines: a commercial-size band saw, a twelve-inch table saw, a hefty radial arm saw, an eight-inch jointer, and a huge surface planer. Hand planes, backsaws, miter boxes, awls, chisels, draw knives, scrapers, punches, auger bits and braces, twist drills and Forstner bits, crosscut and ripsaws, clamps from tiny ones to ten footers, claw hammers, ball peens, mallets, measuring gauges, and rulers hung from the walls or sat on shelves. Grandpa's shop times ten.

Near a door that opened to the outside stood a barrel stove, which is simply a firebox made out of an empty steel barrel placed on its side with a door in the front for loading wood, a few vent holes, and a smokestack running up from the rear. "Barrel stoves give off a lot of heat and are dirt cheap to build," Archie observed. "You ought to get one for that garage of yours. By golly, I may just have one lying around somewhere. Next time you come down, we'll find it."

"It's a deal, Archie," I said.

"Come over here, Deek," Archie said, gesturing to me to follow. "Is this what you're looking for?"

Neatly stacked with spacers evenly placed between seasoning boards was rough-cut ⁵⁄₄ cherry. I was looking at planks an inch and a quarter thick. Sliding a board from the top of the stack, Archie ran his fingertips over the rough surface. "Beautiful, isn't it? It has been seasoning for over a year, probably just about ready to become part of that dining room furniture you're so eager to build," he said, sliding the board back in place.

"You like wood, don't you?" I asked, more in a rhetorical sense than expecting an answer. Archie looked at me quizzically, as if the question struck a nerve.

"Well, that is a question I never thought about. But sure I do, who doesn't? Now, don't get me wrong, I like working with steel but more because that's where I'm needed. There was a real call for skilled machinists in this town when I was growing up, and well, that's where life took me. I ran a gas station and car repair shop way back, too, but machining was my calling and that's where I went, and glad of it, too. But, you asked the question, and yes, I like wood. It's nice to work with. Come on, follow me, I want to show you something."

I followed Archie outside through the door to the right of the barrel stove, down a narrow short sidewalk to the side door of his house. He opened the door. "Lillian, I'm here to show Deek a little of my woodwork. We got our coveralls on, just wanted to warn you." With that, Archie led me through the door and up two steps to the kitchen. Lillian greeted us.

"I see you and Archie have been enjoying yourselves," she said, looking at me.

"We certainly have. It's nice to see you again, Lillian. I guess I'm on the wood tour this time."

"Well, that's one a lot of people never get to see. Archie keeps his woodwork close to home or else he'd get too busy with people wanting him to do that, too."

I felt honored and said so. Pointing to the kitchen cabinets, Archie chimed in, "I made those, and the fireplace mantel, and the tables in the living room over there, and all the paneling on the walls and the floors. Now does that answer your question about my liking wood?"

I was surrounded by beautifully finished cabinets, paneling, and furniture all made of oak and all simple in design, similar to mission style. "Yes, Archie," I said, directing my raised eyes to Lillian. "It sure does."

"Would you boys like some pie?" Lillian asked.

Before I could answer, Archie jumped in, "Nope. Deek here and I have some wood to go through." With that I bid Lillian good-bye and followed Archie back to the woodshop.

Archie's voice and demeanor had softened ever since he entered the woodshop. I guessed from what he and Lillian said that woodworking was his avocational interest while machining was what he did to make a living.

"Here Deek, look at this," Archie said, referring to a planed cherry plank that he retrieved from an orderly arranged scrap pile. "Why, you can see the sunlight just waiting to come out." He turned the board this way and that until sunlight from a dusty window seemed to dance, even on the unfinished surface. Carefully, Archie set the board back on the pile.

When Archie worked with steel, he seldom commented on the aesthetics of what he created. He certainly didn't emote over it as I did. Now and then he would nod proudly at a polished piece of steel that had no scratches, but I never heard him make a comment relevant to its aesthetic quality. Where I saw beauty, he saw function. Obviously, wood was another matter.

"I built my house, Deek. I know every stick in it. This is the third one I built, ground up."

"I thought that you were a machinist, Archie. Where did you get the time and know-how to be a carpenter?"

"And machinists can't build houses? Where did you get that notion? You seem to think that certain people do only certain things. Now, I think differently. Everybody can build a house or run a machine, it's just a matter of figuring and doing. Not as good as I can, but they can do it," Archie said smugly.

"What about training, Archie? A person just doesn't pick up a saw and start cutting."

"Why not, Deek? It's part of who we are. You know, if somebody had to build a house, had no other way of doing it, why, they would build a house."

"A shelter, maybe, Archie, but a house?"

"A house, Deek, four walls and a roof. People do it all the time. There's no mystery to it if you just use your head and pay attention to what gravity is always trying to do."

"I know a lot of people who couldn't build a house if their life depended on it," I countered.

"Well good for them then it doesn't. But that's the reason they can't do it, because they don't have to. Now, pick through that pile of cherry and pick out the boards you want. Do you know what you're looking for, Deek, or do I have to do it for you?" Archie's sarcasm returned as it always seemed to after we talked of anything philosophic in nature.

I didn't answer Archie as I dug through the pile picking some and rejecting others. My eyes were looking for solid grain with no checking. When I had the material that I felt I needed, Archie threw in three more boards, "To cover your mistakes," he said.

"Where did you get this wood, Archie?" I asked.

"From up in my woods," he replied proudly.

"What woods, Archie?"

"My woods, Deek. That's where all the wood for the house came from, too. Now, do you have a surface planer in that shop of yours?"

"No."

"Well, then, we better get this wood in shape so you can get somewhere with it."

Together, Archie and I flattened one side of each of the boards on his jointer. After having left his machine shop only a half hour earlier, the difference in sound struck me. The woodshop machinery was fast and whining, much more menacing than machines in his machine shop, except for the grinder, perhaps. The blades of the heavy, tuned jointer were spinning at a good 5,000 r.p.m., sending high overtones screeching around the shop.

Using the same machine, we placed the smooth, flattened side against the fence and planed a true, ninety-degree edge on each board. Moving to the table saw, we placed the true edge against the saw's fence and ripped the other uneven edge of the boards to square. The final procedure was putting boards through his surface planer, which brought them to a consistent thickness and smoothness all around.

"Nobody ever saw that before, Deek," Archie said, looking at a finished board.

"What didn't they see, Archie?" I asked, unsure of what he was talking about.

"That," Archie said, pointing to the surface of the wood. "Every time you plane a board, you're the first to see what's underneath, what was put there years ago. New every time, always different. It's true, Deek, like so many other things," he concluded, stroking his fingers slowly across the smooth reflective surface of the gleaming cherry and drawing me into yet another of his lessons.

It was clear that working on wood had put Archie in a startlingly expansive mood. He continued.

"I'll tell you one that lots of people don't think about. The inside of an engine. Now, Deek, when I took the motors down from those Model A's, why, the inside was as clean and shiny as if it was just made, all hidden inside a rusty old block of cast iron. And how about the inside of rocks? Same thing."

"And dirt?"

"Always new when you plow it over."

"What do you do with all of the wood chips?" I asked Archie, referring to the mound left at the foot of the planer.

"I take them back up to the woods where they came from. The creatures do all sorts of things with them, even make houses or whatever you want to call them," he answered, as if winning a round of checkers.

After sweeping up, we loaded the finished cherry carefully into Archie's pickup truck, drove to my house, and unloaded the stock into my basement. Looking at my newly constructed workbench and neatly arranged, cleaned, and sharpened tools, Archie observed, "Well, Deek, it looks like you're ready to go. Let me see that plane over there?" he said, pointing to my Bailey No. 5. He held the plane upside down and looked across its sole. "Next time you come down to the shop, bring this with you, and the other two as well. I'll get those soles back in shape."

"My pleasure, Archie. What do I owe you for the wood?"

"A good-looking cabinet, Deek, one that you're proud of. Besides, you did a good job at painting the lathe. I guess that's a fair swap."

"Your woods, Archie? It must be some woods," I commented as we drove back to his place.

"Yup, it is," he replied. "It sure is."

# 5 · *The China Cabinet*

*A designer will stress the creative aspects, but if he also knows how to build, his design will be the better for it.*

Norm Abrams, *Measure Twice, Cut Once*, 1996

When it comes to designing furniture, I rate myself about a three on a scale of ten. What I see in my mind's eye never quite makes it to paper in the same way. To make matters worse, whenever I do draw plans, I find it difficult to stick to them. This has led to as many disasters as it has to enlightened pieces, so I figure it all equals out over the long run. But I was determined not to play the averages with my china cabinet. I wasn't about to wager with some precious cherry. I wanted to end up with a piece that was practical and well built.

There are numerous plans that can be purchased for making furniture, but I don't like working from store-bought plans. The combination of being poor at design and reluctant to use someone else's plans led me to a solution that I have relied on for years: I go to furniture stores, find a piece that I like, take some measurements, change a few things that suit me, make a set of plans, and build. Since there were no furniture stores per se in Ladysmith (although some furniture could be found at a few stores, including the local hardware store), Bonnie and I headed to the Twin Cities.

Minneapolis–Saint Paul is about 125 miles west of Ladysmith, a relatively easy one-day turnaround trip. But, for me, this wasn't going to be an easy trip. I find going to furniture stores depressing. Besides the annoying salespeople, I think that most of the furniture is terrible—production-line veneered flakeboard stuff that does nothing to enlighten the human spirit. We visited five stores, or "marts," as some of them were called, before finding one that had a good collection of beautifully made Quaker-style furniture. Zeroing in on a china closet that fit the concept I had in mind, I set about taking measurements, but, to my dismay, I had forgotten my tape measure.

Since I didn't need accurate measurements, I called out thumb measurements as Bonnie jotted them down. The china cabinet was to be twenty-seven thumbs wide, ten thumbs deep, and just a bit higher than my head. With a rough sketch and relative measurements, we headed home.

Knowing that my thumb measures one and a quarter inches from its end to its first knuckle, and that I stand five feet eleven inches, I began converting thumbs to inches and laying out a set of plans. I changed the design from the two-door configuration displayed in the furniture store to three smaller doors, and instead of paneled doors for the base of the cabinet, I decided to use solid wood doors, confident that they wouldn't warp if I joined them correctly.

Taking advantage of the college's summer schedule, I became engrossed in the project. The wood that Archie had given me had sat the requisite few weeks in my basement shop to become acclimated to the prevailing conditions. Like steel, wood responds to temperature changes, although it does so at a much slower rate and for quite different reasons. With steel, its molecules respond rather quickly to temperature changes by either sitting still when cooled or jumping about when warmed. This molecular movement accounts for expansion or contraction in steel. With wood, temperature has a more indirect bearing. Warmer temperatures hold more moisture than do colder ones and it is moisture or the lack of it that swells or shrinks wood, and that takes time. Because of this, it is wise to keep a shop at a steady temperature and an even level of humidity. Since no two places are equal in that regard, it makes sense to let seasoned wood sit for a week or so in the shop before cutting it to size. Grandpa had another way of approaching the subject. "It's best to be in a place for a while before you go changing things. Don't go cutting things up until it's time." He concluded his lecture, which I heard numerous times when I joined him on his shop visits, "You understand that?" He never waited for an answer.

I began my project by laying out the cherry to study its color and grain. In cherry, matching color is as important as matching grain because, over time, the color of cherry deepens to varying shades from cinnamon to a deep red paprika. The extra time it takes to lay out the boards is well spent when you consider it an investment in beauty. There are few things more beautiful than aged cherry.

Thankfully, Archie had made sure that the edge of each board was perfectly square, an absolute requirement for gluing up stock, and since I didn't have a jointer in my shop, a real time and ego saver. I guess that I could have hand-planed the edges, but when it comes to getting a perfect edge, I know my limits.

It takes strong, unforgiving, heavy and, above all (or so it seems to me) cumbersome clamps to squeeze glue-coated edges of wood together. Mine were four feet long, made of black pipe with a heavy steel tailstop on one end and a screw fixture that moved a sliding head on the other. The first requirement was to adjust the tailstop so that the space between it and the screw head approximate the combined width of the boards. The second was to place the glued boards in the clamps and turn the screw tight until the adhesive oozed from the joints. It may sound simple enough, but for me, clamping is never done without banged shins, glue-covered hands and clothes, and a generous application of foul words. This time was no different.

While the glue set, I made the three upper frames for the door. Unlike gluing, I like making frames, especially using mortise and tenon joints, the kind I selected for my cabinet. Made correctly, the tenon is cut to fit snugly into a slot, or mortise, which is chiseled out of a corresponding piece of wood. Fully equipped shops, an oxymoron if there ever was one, include a mortising machine, or at least a drill press with a mortising attachment. I had neither, so I used a chisel and that made cutting the mortises a pleasure.

Because I had decided on a design that required a face frame in addition to the three door frames, my mallet and three-eighths-inch chisel kept me going for the better part of two days measuring and cutting twenty-two mortises. I then turned to my table saw and, using a jig I specifically designed for the purpose, cut the corresponding tenons. When the task was completed, I had set aside neat stacks of carefully labeled cut lumber ready for gluing, squaring, and clamping.

Archie's extra boards came in handy when, after the frames were squared and glued, I dropped one. One of its corners landed squarely on the unforgiving concrete floor of the basement, sending out a sound like a rifle shot that echoed off the concrete block basement walls. This was not an honest mistake like those that occur from misreading a ruler mark. This was an error that falls under the category of "haste makes waste," born out of excitement at seeing the cabinet emerging from a stack of boards. Despite my occasional mistakes, however, the cabinet was slowly taking shape.

The rough boards that Archie had seasoned in his woodshop were taking on a new reality, one that would weave itself tightly into the life of my family, just as my grandfather's dining room suite of furniture did for his. This cabinet would hold and display dishes that would dress a table that I hoped to build someday as well, and I envisioned it being passed down through my family, its glistening contents storing memories like the wood stored sunlight. It is my nature to emote over certain things that I do and making furniture for my home is one of them—probably a lingering gene or two taking me back to days when my ancestral bucks built or did without.

Given the size of the boards and the look of the grain, I guessed that the wood came from more than one tree. I wondered about Archie's woods and was hopeful of seeing the spot the lumber came from. All in good time, I thought as I laid out the material in preparation for final assembly.

This was the easiest part of the job and, next to making tight-fitting joints, the most rewarding. Some glue, screws, a few nails, and eight hinges later (the middle of the three top doors was fixed into position) the cabinet stood before me, from tree to timber to lumber to cabinet.

Until a finish is applied, it is difficult to imagine the beauty that lies hidden in wood. No matter how many times I finish wood, I am always overwhelmed by the look that comes from the finishing process. It is a sanctified moment.

Following the same procedure for finishing that my grandfather taught me to use, I started the process by using a cabinet scraper. If there was ever a description that didn't match process, it is "cabinet scraper." The euphony of the word "scraper" suggests fingernails on a blackboard rather than the pleasant sound of crisp steel playing happily on the surface of forgiving wood. I wish there were another word to describe the process, like cabinet caresser or wood smoother, but cabinet scraper it is. Wood finished using this simple device, made of a flat piece of ground steel sharpened by curling its edge, takes on a sheen, and my new cabinet glistened with each stroke of the misnamed tool.

As I gingerly took my scraper from its protective sleeve I took note of the tool's cold steel; the bracing feel reminded me of reluctance, like a nervous lover, perhaps. As I worked the scraper over the cherry, it warmed not only on my hands but to its own work. Its molecules excited, the flat piece of steel seemed more and more eager to do what it was made to do. There was a point when I felt myself and the scraper join forces, our energy bouncing back and forth in perpetual motion. Needing to reposition the work, I set the scraper down on top of the workbench, opened the vise, and readjusted the wood. Not looking, I reached for the tool again, but my hand touched another that was sitting nearby. Instantly, the cold of the setting scraper sent an alarm signal almost as if it were an electric shock. Surprised, I looked down and welcomed back the one I had been using. This is the way of tools. No matter how often we use them or how deeply we become attached to them, once set on the rack or placed in a drawer, they separate from us. I, however, had not separated from them. In my mind, the tools were simply waiting, like beloved pets, for my return.

I followed Grandpa's recipe, which included a prefinish routine of wetting down the wood to raise its grain and giving it a final, light sanding when it dried. Then I applied my first coat of finish, made from a mixture of two parts boiled linseed oil with one part mineral spirits heated until it felt warm but not hot. According to my grandfather, you hand-rub this mixture into the surface once a day for a week, once a week for a month, then once a month for a year. There were probably easier and just as effective ways of finishing cherry, but by doing it this way I was touching base with Grandpa while enjoying the sensuous feeling of rubbing warm oil on bone-smooth, glistening cherry. The first coat of oil slowly disappeared into the thirsty cherry. Following Grandpa's formula, I would add another warm coat tomorrow. It was time to turn my attention to making the shelves.

China cabinets are places to hold light, which, even on gloomy days, needs to dance about unrestricted. I recalled the delightful clarity of Grandpa's china cabinet, in which the glass-and dishware seemed to float on rays of light, an illusion he created by having glass sides and shelves. I had elected to use solid sides but determined early on that I would use glass shelves—special glass shelves made from the glass I wrestled from the swollen front door of the flooded Wilkes-Barre home.

At the time of the flood, I had no idea what I would do with thick, beveled, greenish tinted glass, I just knew that to toss it on the pile of flood debris growing on the front curb would be profane. It was, after all, a front door, and that in itself made it sacred to me.

The notion of using the treasured glass for shelves in my china cabinet came to mind late in the design stage. Once I made the commitment, I adjusted the dimensions I pirated from Minneapolis accordingly. Fortunately, only slight adjustments were necessary in the width to ensure that three shelves could be cut from the glass. With the heavy glass safely strapped into the back seat of my car, I drove to a glass shop in Eau Claire, about sixty miles south of Ladysmith, where a young craftsman waited to take on the job.

Finding a glass cutter willing to take on the risky job of cutting the old, brittle glass was a chore in itself. I had called every glass cutter I could find and finally settled on the fellow in Eau Claire, who responded to my inquiry with, "Sounds like a real challenge. I sure would like to give it my best shot. Old glass is special, you know." All of the others stopped after saying, "I can't promise anything," a phrase without a clarifier that sends me running.

Carefully laying the old glass on a soft, mat-covered bench, the young craftsman laid down the lines, put a straight edge in place, and deftly slid a lubricated glass cutter along the brittle surface. A hissing sound rose in protest. With practiced skill, he tapped along the line, then placed a thin, steel slat under the glass on the back edge of the scored line. With a quick move, he split the glass. One more expert cut, and I had three beautiful shelves with bevels ready to face front.

Relieved, I said to the young man, "Great job. You sure do good work."

"Thanks," he responded. "I wasn't sure it would work, but it sure did, didn't it? Boy, that's nice glass. Where did you get it?" he asked passionately.

I told the young man the story of salvaging the glass from the Wilkes-Barre home and that I had moved it with me to Wisconsin.

"You did the right thing. Too many people throw good things away," he said, with youthful authority. Before I left the shop, I had the young man cut me three pieces of one-eighth-inch glass for the top three doors.

Back in my shop, with the glass securely in place and the cabinet complete, I called up the basement stairs, "Bonnie, come here, I want to show you something." There was no mystery here. Bonnie had seen me working on the cabinet, but the finished product was different. When she appeared, I stood there like a fully fanned peacock, unabashedly proud of what I had made. Like most every other man I know who makes things for around the house, the first person I wanted to see my work was the woman in my life. Perhaps it's those ancestral bucks' genes again, needing to prove to my lady that I could build whatever she needed to make life better. Whatever it is that causes it, that's what I do.

"Beautiful," she said. "I love it."

"Pretty good, huh?"

"Oh, it's wonderful. I love the shelves."

"From the front door of the Wilkes-Barre house."

"Yes, I know," she said girlishly. "You must have told me about it a dozen times."

"I made a few mistakes but you can hardly see them," I confessed.

"I don't see any," Bonnie said knowingly. "I think it's perfect."

Following some hugs and kisses, we lugged the cabinet from the basement to its rightful place in the dining room, where, sharing the room with the cabinet I had built nine years earlier, my young family celebrated.

# 6 · Visiting the Truck

*They must remember that it is not the trade that evaluates the man, but it is rather the man that dignifies the pursuit or calling; and that muscular power, though very good in its place, is not the most essential requisite of an engineer, but that the cultivation of the mind is the first step towards eminence in any trade or profession.*

Stephen Roper, *A Catechism of High Pressure or Noncondensing Steam Engines,* 1874

With college in recess and the days lengthening with the arrival of summer, my Saturday morning visits to Archie's shop grew to include weekday and evening visits. On more than one occasion, Lillian had invited me into their home, which she kept immaculate. From casual observation, it also occurred to me that she ruled the roost; while Archie had his shop, this was Lillian's domain. Sitting in his house, Archie was taciturn, given to looking at television or perusing any number of tool and equipment catalogs that sat neatly stacked to the side of his chair. Lillian, on the other hand, was eager to converse and enjoy company.

With the finished china cabinet sitting in its rightful place, I decided to take the opportunity to invite Archie and Lillian to our house to have a look. Whereas I had become a regular visitor to Archie's shop and home, for one reason or another, my invitation to them in reciprocation went unfulfilled. Coming to see the cabinet would, I hope, change that.

In the early evening, I drove up to Archie and Lillian's house expecting a casual visit. Archie was bent over fiddling with the doorknob of his side door. My "hello, Archie" was greeted with a grunt. From his surly manner, it was evident that he was upset. He was usually calm and in control, so this edgy and unpleasant fellow standing before me was an entirely new sight.

"What's wrong, Archie?"

Not looking up, he said, "I have work to do."

"You want some help?"

Still looking away, he answered curtly, "Nope. If I did, I'd ask."

Archie turned a new doorknob over in his hands. "Some newfangled idea cooked up by some damned fool who doesn't know the first damn thing about anything."

This was the first time that I had heard Archie curse, and as mild as it was, it startled me.

I felt awkward simply standing there but to turn and leave didn't feel right. Besides, my curiosity was piqued. I had seen Archie work long hours making parts that, if they didn't turn out to his liking, he set aside and began anew without a curse or a harsh word. He did raise his voice a few times in the shop, but never at work, only at people.

I watched for a few minutes then noticed a folded set of directions lying on the floor. I picked it up. "Archie, according to this, all you need to do is push that metal tab in with a screwdriver, then slide it into that slot," I said assuredly.

Archie rose up like an angry bear, looking at me with the knob held in his large left hand, held back as if he was either going to throw it at me or use it as a weapon. Instinctively, I drew back.

Adjusting his posture to a less threatening stance, he reached out with the doorknob, "Here, if you know so goddamn much, you fix it. Goddamn teacher knows every goddamn thing there is to know." He shoved the knob into my hand, turned, and disappeared noisily into the house.

"What is this goddamn teacher business?" I yelled after him. Archie's sarcastic references to my being a teacher finally caused me to boil over. The evening fell silent as I stood by the open door with the knob in my hand. Perhaps out of spite, I picked up the old, wooden-handled screwdriver that Archie had set to one side and, following the simple directions, put the knob in place within a few seconds. "There, you son of a bitch," I thought, turning the doorknob back and forth to signal triumph with its chattering latch. The anger I had felt mixed with afterthought and I wished that the scene had never occurred. I wanted to ring the doorbell and reason things out, but instead, I turned and walked with quickening steps toward my car.

"Dick," I heard softly. "Dick, wait a moment."

It was Lillian's soft voice.

"I'm sorry for this," she said sincerely. "You just don't know. Archie can be very mean. There are things that you don't know. I can't stay out here, it's best you leave, but try to understand."

Acknowledging her sympathetic remarks, I simply said, "Thank you, Lillian," got into my car, and drove the short distance home. Understand what? Of course, here I was standing in the threshold of a man's house telling him how to fix the latch that keeps the world at bay—a proud craftsman, a machinist. That in itself placed me in jeopardy. I had broken a rule that a man should never break. I offered to help when I wasn't asked—not by word, not by gesture, or by tone. Perhaps I had become too familiar, treating Archie as an old friend, when in fact, I had known him for only about six weeks. I included myself in Archie's domain, and it was clearly a mistake. I felt terrible.

By the time I put my car away and headed into the house, my transgression blossomed, my head and heart arguing about what to do next. The phone rang. It was Lillian. She apologized for Archie's outburst and hoped that it would not prevent me from visiting again.

"No apology necessary, Lillian. It was my fault. I had no right telling Archie how to fix anything. I hope I can mend the fence."

"Archie can get pretty touchy if you push him the wrong way. What exactly happened out there, anyway?" Lillian asked.

I told Lillian the story about the doorknob and my finding the directions.

"Oh, that would have done it all right," she said, with a tone suggesting that she had seen it all before.

"Well, Lillian, I don't want this to get in the way. What do you suggest?" I asked earnestly.

The other end of the phone was quiet for a moment, then Lillian said, "I'm only telling you this because Archie seems to like you and I think it's good for him that you are in the shop. He's not getting any younger. But please don't tell him or anybody what I'm going to tell you." Lillian paused as if waiting for my assurance that our discussion was private.

"Lillian, I won't say a word, I promise."

"Well, you were in the wrong to push yourself on Archie, but there's more to it than that," she said with authority. Her voice then changed to a near whisper that was laced with sincerity and regret. "Archie can't read. Not a word. He gets very angry at anyone that questions his way of doing things. I guess he felt that's what you were doing."

Having worked alongside Archie, I never would have guessed that he couldn't read. "Lillian, this is hard to believe. You mean that Archie is illiterate?"

"Well, now," she said, her voice strengthened, "I don't like that word because I don't think it fits. I'd rather just say that Archie can't read. He just can't put words together. Why, you being a teacher and all . . ." Her voice trailed off. I remained silent. "They didn't treat him right in school, the little he went there. His older sister, Rose, used to read him his lessons, and Archie, well, you know what kind of brain he has, memorized her reading and took it to school acting like he could read. He just got tired of it and quit before the eighth grade—been on his own ever since." Her tone tinged with regret, she added, "He never forgot it or forgave his teachers. And you being a teacher, well, I hope you can understand."

"This clears up a lot. But what do you think Lillian? Where do I go from here?"

"You know, Archie doesn't get close to very many people and you know how he is when someone gets him angry. But with you, I think that he'll put all this aside. He likes you. If he didn't, why, he never would let you work in his shop. And giving you the wood," she said with a laugh, "why, it's a rare thing for Archie to be giving things to anybody." Returning to a more serious tone, Lillian continued, "Now, he won't make the first move, I'm sure of that."

"I'm ready to do that, Lillian," I assured her. "What do you suggest?"

"I think it best if you just come down to the shop just like you've been doing."

"Is tomorrow soon enough?"

"Well, probably not. I know that Archie is planning to go to Saint Paul for some steel. Why don't you stop by the truck on Friday night? That would be a perfect time."

"The truck?" I asked, confused.

"Of course, you don't know about that. Well, every Friday night, Archie and I go downtown and park the truck on Miner Avenue to receive visitors."

"You do?"

"Oh yes, been doing it for years. It's a good way to stay in touch with people. As I was saying, why don't you come downtown and pay us a visit? I'm sure that Archie will open the window for you."

"Open the window?"

"Archie only opens the window to people he wants to talk with. He'll open for you, I'm sure."

More than curious, but not willing to push farther, I simply asked, "What time?"

"We're always there between seven and eight-thirty. Come down around eight or so."

Our conversation ended with Lillian repeating her apology. I thanked her and promised that I would be downtown on Friday night.

Lillian's disclosure cleared up a lot that had been bothering me, especially Archie's negative references to my being a teacher. He had reasons to dislike the profession, of that I was now sure. But I was not going to let his unfortunate experiences, whatever they might be, get in the way of a growing friendship, a friendship that I needed, and from what Lillian said, Archie did as well.

As I do whenever I'm bothered by something, I headed for my shop, where I spent an hour or so cleaning up and putting my tools in order for whatever project came next.

On Friday night I headed for downtown Ladysmith to visit Archie's truck to apologize for my arrogance. I wasn't sure where downtown I would find Archie, but being that the shopping area was essentially confined to two blocks or so along Miner Avenue, I was sure that I would spot him. I parked near the power company office on the south side of Miner and began walking east along the sedate but busy business section of town. Passing Fedde's Bar, a favorite haunt for Friday night fun, I was greeted by some of my college students, who tried to get me to join them in a game of pool. Mark Rucker, one of my voice students, was particularly interested in getting me into a contest of eight ball, since every time we played that's exactly where he kept me. But as Archie already had me in that position, I took a rain check and continued on my search.

A short time later, I stood in front of the Security State Bank to scan the next and final block of downtown and spotted Archie's truck parked in front of the JCPenney store, which was near the end of the block on the opposite side of the street. I decided to observe the comings and goings, waiting for an opportune time to make my approach. One couple after another, the woman going to Lillian's side and the man going to Archie's, stopped by, chatted, and went on their way. No one seemed to linger too long, and the odd visiting rite appeared more formal than casual. In the ten or so minutes that I stood on the corner, Archie had not closed his window at all, so I guessed that he was pleased with the line of well-wishers. That boded well for me, I thought, and continued east on Miner Avenue, although my steps were slower. Another couple appeared for a visit and I ducked into the Ace Hardware store. I wasn't ready for Archie to spot me, nor did I want some well-intentioned fellow inadvertently cutting in as I made my approach to his truck. When I stepped out of the hardware store, Archie's window was up, and there was no one that appeared to be heading his way. I couldn't make out Lillian, whose view was hidden behind the reflective light bouncing off the windshield.

I slowly crossed Miner Avenue on a diagonal, giving Archie plenty of opportunity to recognize my approach. His window remained closed and he sat immovable, looking straight out the windshield. I was convinced that he could see me, but there was no indication from him that, in fact, he did. Moments before I reached the driver's side of the door, the window slowly lowered.

"Well, look who's here," Archie dug right in. "How come you're not out fixing doorknobs, or did you give that up?"

"No more doorknobs, Archie. Actually, when I saw your truck parked here, I decided to come over and apologize."

"For what, sticking your nose into places where it doesn't belong?"

"Yes, I guess you can put it that way. I had no right to interfere and I'm sorry. I'd like to put it aside."

"Oh," he said, turning his face toward me, "it's aside all right, so is that doorknob of yours."

"What do you mean?" I asked earnestly. "Did it break again?"

"Nope, didn't have a chance. I took it out and made a new one the way it should be. I should have done that from the beginning, the way things are made today. You want it?" he asked slyly, with a touch of humor.

"No, I have no use for it."

"Good, because I threw it in the junk. No good to anybody anyway." Archie's demeanor relaxed and he shifted his body, placing his arm on the bottom frame of the truck's window. "What have you been doing with yourself?" he asked in a friendly voice.

"Besides working around the house, I finished the cabinet."

"You don't say, I was wondering about that. Been a few weeks hasn't it?"

"Three to be exact. It worked out pretty well. Why don't you and Lillian stop by to take a look at it?"

"You need to talk to Lillian about that," he said. "She makes the visiting plans, not me."

I looked past Archie to see Lillian busy talking with a couple who stopped by on her side of the truck. "It looks like Lillian's busy," I observed. "I'll drop by later."

"Better yet," Archie offered, "why don't you come down to the shop tomorrow morning? I could use your help."

"Well, I guess I could do that," I said pensively to hide my eagerness. "What time?"

Instead of answering my question, he turned his eyes to a fellow who had come up behind me. "Hello, Carl, what have you been doing?" he said to the man. Then turning to me, "See you tomorrow, Deek."

I left Archie's truck and headed into the Coast to Coast Hardware store that sat right next to JCPenney's and bought some sabre saw blades. By the time I came out, Archie's truck was nowhere to be seen.

I made my way back to my car via Fedde's, where Mark sunk the eight once again.

# 7 · The Woods

*Whether it be the few remaining virgin deciduous areas in the eastern United States, the great stands of the sequoia in California, the rain forest in the lower Ho River valley in Washington, the Circassian forests of the Caspian Sea area, the timber reserves for the construction of the Ise Shrine, or the timberline along the upper reaches of the mountainous regions of the world, there is an aura of maturity, a sense of conflict ended.*

George Nakashima, *The Soul of a Tree, A Woodworker's Reflections*, 1981

I found peace traveling the gravel roads that crisscrossed Rusk County. From Ladysmith, I could go in any direction and within a few miles find gravel roads that placed me shoulder to shoulder with farm fields, timber stands, ponds, lakes, rivers, creeks, and tiny hamlets. It was not unusual to drive fifty or more miles and not touch blacktop.

Even though Archie's shop was just a mile from my house, blacktop all the way, now and then I drove north on Route 27 for about five miles, then, turning east and south, made my way to Archie's shop on unpaved roads. I was on gravel now, where the subtle slip and slide gave me a feeling of steering a boat through water. Yawing my way along over the crispy, dry road, it felt good to meander instead of just heading straight to his shop. I had promised myself that I would take Lillian's advice and simply act as if I had no awareness of Archie's inability to read, a promise that would require considerable discipline on my part, as I was very curious to know how he had accumulated so much knowledge. From my own experience around skilled craftsmen, I could understand how he acquired skills at machining and woodworking without the aid of the written word; after all, practice, a keen eye for observation, and a good mind ensured some degree of success at making and fixing things. But there was more to Archie than skill.

The sound of a stone zinging around the fender was good accompaniment to my thoughts about Archie. My world of higher education was built on reading, writing, and libraries filled to overflowing. Words were a big part of my business. The question of how Archie had done all of the things he did—how he amassed technical information, interpreted drawings, kept abreast of new developments, invented, and created, stirred in me. I had enough experience with teaching to know that talent means very little if there isn't a whole lot of determination behind it. Referring to skilled craftsmen, my grandfather would say ninety percent work, ten percent talent. I reasoned that what made Archie special was his ability, through practiced and acquired skill, to bring a thought to reality. The most lofty thought in the world dies on the vine if it can't be expressed. It makes little difference whether it's musical thought or machinery thought. What truly matters is being able to express it, having the skill to get it out there, words or no words. My car suddenly jerked from the float of gravel to unyielding blacktop. I was close to Archie's shop. My mind switched to the prospect of our continued friendship.

The door to the shop was wide open, and as I stepped from my dusty car, I could hear the rumbling sound of Archie's large lathe. I had learned long ago to never approach a person working with machinery, as a sudden interruption could trigger a serious accident. Heeding this rule, I peered quietly into the shop to see light cast by the small, focused lamp that hung over Archie's lathe catching silvery satiny pieces of twirling steel. The shadows created by the downcast light gave the appearance that Archie's hands and forearms came from the lathe rather than from his torso, which remained in heavy gray shadow.

Archie's left hand reached for the switch that controlled the lathe, and with a simultaneous move of his head, his eyes caught me standing in the doorway. "Good afternoon, Deek, or is it morning? Never thought you'd make it here today." I stepped through the door to be greeted with the friendly aroma of work.

"I took the long way around. What are you making?"

"It's a piece I'm making for Harry. Why do you want to know?" Archie asked.

"Just curious, Archie. Who is Harry?" I asked.

"Now, let's see, Deek, you've been here for about two minutes and in that time you've asked two questions. That's over ten thousand questions a week. Too many for me. Just to keep you quiet for a minute, I don't know what I'm making for Harry, I just know what he wants. And Harry—why, he's an airplane mechanic that lives up by my woods. Now, can I get back to work?" Archie said with a note of finality, but then added, "By the way, that part you needed is behind the door. I'd like to get it out of here. Besides, your lawn looks terrible."

I rummaged through the pile to find the lawn mower part that I left with Archie a few weeks earlier. Attached was a piece of masking tape with $2 written in heavy pencil. Archie never did machine work for free, and even though I helped Archie around the shop, I had no qualms about his charging me. There was a clear line between my working with Archie and his doing work for me, we both understood that. I stepped out the door to take the part to my car.

"What are you doing out there?" I heard Archie call. "I could use your help."

I went back into the shop and handed Archie two dollars.

"Thanks," he said, putting the bills in his fat wallet—Archie always carried a lot of cash. "Well, now, why don't you set up the miller? We need to cut a key way in this shaft."

"How wide?"

"A quarter inch."

"Have you talked to Lillian about coming up to see the cabinet?" I asked.

"Yup, but first let's get the work done."

In less than a half hour we were finished, and I was heading to my house with Archie and Lillian following behind in his pickup.

"Well, what do you think, Archie?" I asked as we looked at the cabinet.

"Why is it sitting on all that paper?" he asked, making no comment about the construction. I explained my grandfather's finishing process. "Pretty old-fashioned way of doing things. That's an odd way you attached the frame to the sides, that's for sure," he said, observing that I had decided to insert the face frame between the cabinet sides rather than over its edges, which is a more conventional approach. "But I guess that's what you wanted to do, so I guess it's okay with me. Where did you get those shelves?"

"Left over from the flood," I replied, telling him about the swollen front door.

Lillian, who was standing quietly to one side, turned to Bonnie. "Archie told me about you folks going through that awful time. I'm glad that you're here, away from all that mess. I bet you like your new house."

"It's wonderful," Bonnie replied. "The winter was pretty rough, but in some ways, it was the most beautiful winter I've ever seen. Is it always so cold?"

"I remember colder. Isn't that right?" Lillian directed to Archie.

"Yup. Do you think I ought to show Deek the mother of his cabinet?" Archie said, breaking away from winter weather.

I looked at Lillian. Mother! It turned out that this was Archie's way of inviting me to see his woods. Bonnie was invited, too, but she couldn't go because of the children's violin lessons.

We wanted them to stay for lunch, but Archie was clearly eager to leave. After a little more chatter, Archie cut things short by stating matter-of-factly, "We have work to do." He then directed his words to Lillian. "The bus is leaving, so unless you want to walk, it's time to go."

Archie was not very sociable in any house other than his own and even there, he seemed to struggle with conversation. Perhaps that's why he enjoyed visiting people while seated in his truck; he could always drive away. His visits to people's homes were always cut short, usually with the phrase, "the bus is leaving." As gruff as it may seem, Lillian always complied, knowing how uncomfortable it was for Archie to engage in relaxed conversation. For those who knew him, Archie's discomfort with social mores was simply understood as part of who he was, an acceptable quirk that added to rather than detracted from his personality. To some degree, I envied Archie in this regard. I had moved too much, been too often a newcomer for my own quirks to be seen as a facet of my character. Especially in this part of the world, a newcomer's eccentricities are best kept hidden, lest they be seen as flaws.

In less than fifteen minutes, Archie and I were heading to his famed woods. He drove his truck like he drove his Model A, slightly hunched over the wheel, which he held cautiously in both hands. Top speed was 40 m.p.h.

County Road J veered west, away from the Flambeau, then headed due north. We were backtracking along the road I had taken earlier in the day when I drove to Archie's shop. This time, blacktop changed to gravel as we traveled north for about eight miles, then turned on Girod Road for one mile before heading north again on Fedyn Road, which, after about four miles, dead-ended smack-dab in the midst of wild north country woods. Archie pulled up to a sturdy iron gate and stopped the truck. "Wait here, Deek, I'll open the gate," Archie said as he reached for his ring of keys.

Once through the silver-painted gate, which had Archie's craftsmanship all over it, we cut sharply to the left on a dirt road then down a steep grade to a grassy area where Archie stopped the truck, set the brake, and turned off the motor. To my right was a rustic, cedar-covered cabin with a corrugated tin roof, the same kind of roof that Archie used on his shop. "This is it. My woods," Archie proclaimed as he got out of the truck. I followed.

A slight mist hung in the air of the cloudy day. The woods were cool and perfumed; the sweet smell of early summer. An occasional bird flew from tree to tree, but with the exception of a *chic-a-dee-dee-dee* and a few raspy words from a territorial jay, the woods were bathed in a hushed quiet. To my left, I heard the sound of soft, gurgling water. I walked across mown grass that connected the dirt-covered lane with the cabin and outbuildings, which included four garages, a shed, and a privy. At the edge of the lawn was a twenty-foot drop to where the Thornapple River rushed by.

"See those rocks down there, Deek?" Archie said, pointing to a line of heavy rocks that created small rapids. "I put them there so the water would sing loud enough to be heard up here. Why have a river going by if you can't hear it?"

A picnic table with a heavy iron tube frame, obviously Archie's handiwork, topped with thick white oak boards and benches, sat under a large pine tree. Archie went to one of the sheds and retrieved a dried ear of corn. As he walked to the picnic bench, he pinched off some kernels, dropping them on the ground. In less than a minute, chipmunks were following Archie's trail. "Come over here, Deek, and sit down." Once seated, Archie handed me some corn kernels. Following his lead, I held the kernels on my flattened palm, which I had resting upward on the top of the picnic table. One bold chipmunk suddenly appeared, scurried over to Archie's open palm, grabbed a few kernels, and quickly dashed to the edge of the table with puffed cheeks. In a few minutes, more chipmunks appeared. It was the first time a wild creature ate from my hand.

"Well, let's take a look at the woods," Archie said as he walked over to one of the garages. Undoing a small padlock, he opened the opposing swinging doors of the one-stall clapboard-sided garage. I was greeted by what appeared to be a very modified version of a Model A. I remained outside as Archie squeezed in beside the machine, reached under one side of the raised hood, and connected the battery. "I always disconnect the battery in case one of those creatures decides to chew through a wire," he commented. Climbing into a high seat, he jiggled this and that, and within seconds the sweet sound of a Model A engine reached my ears. Putting the transmission in gear, which protested with a gear-grinding noise, Archie brought the machine into the soft, misty daylight. A stage entrance fit for a king.

The machine looked like it came directly out of a "Gasoline Alley" cartoon, a fantastic, comical, earthy machine. Formerly a 1930 Ford Model A fire truck that served the town of Winter, Wisconsin, a small community thirty miles north of Ladysmith, Archie had modified the machine specifically for use in his woods. He dubbed it "The Weasel."

To accommodate the many twists and turns of various trails that ran through the woods, he reduced the wheel base by cutting about four feet out of the fire engine's middle, then welded the two ends back together. He modified the back into a small pickup truck–like bed with rough-sawn, heavy, white oak planks. The windshield was removed, replaced by a grab bar that was securely fastened to the outside edge of the cowling, a welcome addition, I was soon to learn, to anyone sitting in the passenger seat. There were no springs on the rear end of the Weasel, which was bolted directly to the heavy rear axle. Wrapped in sturdy chains, the rear tires were as large as those found on small farm tractors. A sizable hydraulic arm that was capable of lifting heavy timber or, when modified for winter use, a large, home-made snowplow, protruded from the front like the horn of a rhinoceros. Hidden under a movable plank in the oak bed at the rear of the Weasel, Archie had fashioned a massive winch that he used to pull hefty logs and other objects out of the woods. The Weasel's former identity as a fire engine was transformed into a one-of-a-kind, entirely functional machine.

"C'mon, Deek, hop in."

Hopping in was more like climbing and crawling, but soon I was stationed high up on seats that appeared to be original. Bits of horsehair could be seen sticking through a spot here and there in the worn, tufted, black leather seat. Archie engaged the clutch, and the machine lurched forward, eager to get into the woods. We drove up the steep grade of the lane we had entered only twenty minutes earlier, then made a cut into an almost imperceptible road that led into thick, dark, shaded woods. In first gear, the Weasel's idling engine provided enough power to move the machine effortlessly along at a walking pace. Archie and Weasel were one, just like he was with his big lathe. Man and machine in their element. I, on the other hand, felt as if my backbone was about to come soaring out like a jack-in-the-box, as each bump and grind sent vibrations directly from the uneven ground to my hips, up my spine, and out through my bobbing head.

The steady sound of heavy, thick, clinking chains reminded me that the large right rear wheel was turning within arm's reach of where I sat. I kept both hands clasped tightly around the conveniently placed solid steel grab bar. White knuckles. As I bounced about, Archie sat calmly in his seat like a seasoned horseman mounted on a rambunctious steed.

The road intersected with others that ran off into the shaded woods. I quickly lost my sense of direction on the twisting road, feeling as if I were traveling through a medieval maze. The road had obviously been carved out of the woods with great care and deep respect for the trees that lined its twisting edges. The Weasel's stunted wheelbase and narrow width allowed it to squeeze between large trees that seemed to slap the machine into sharp turns in the road. Left, left again, right, then just past a four-way intersection, Archie brought the Weasel to a halt, and with practiced ease, slid from his high seat to the ground, the engine left to idle. Taking the cue, I uncurled my fingers from the grab bar and awkwardly dropped to the black, moist ground.

"This way, Deek."

By the time I gained my footing, Archie was already walking ten or more paces ahead. His walk was different than I remembered it being around his shop and property. His gait seemed lighter, his arms peacefully at his sides. I followed along the narrow lane in a silence so deep that I could hear the subtle movement of my feet adjusting to the earthen floor. As Archie purposefully walked out in front, I stopped to look at an extraordinary tree that spread its gray, new-leaved branches over a bed of high, yellow grass. Had it not been for the forest that surrounded me, I could have just as well been on an African savannah where one tree commanded all it could survey.

As I stood, Archie backtracked to where I was standing. "It's a Thornapple tree, the namesake for the river." Lightly tugging the edge of a twig, Archie brought a pliable limb to eye level. "See those thorns? They protect its buds. Not many creatures want to run around these branches." Moving away from the tree, we walked side by side along the lane for a short distance when Archie stopped and pointed to a stump.

"There it is. That's the mother of your cabinet with the frame in the wrong place," punctuating the ending with his humorous, high-pitched giggle. The stump sat in an open spot surrounded by the same yellow grass that lay beneath the Thornapple. But instead of having a backdrop of brush and undergrowth, the stump was framed by a background of tall, stately hemlocks—I was standing in a woodland grotto, quiet, sacred, scented by the subtle smell of warm, damp pine.

I walked to the stump as if approaching a saint and bent down to touch its softening top. Years back, my grandfather, who passed his love of trees on to me, told me how the Leni-Lenape (meaning "true men") Indians would place a ring of tobacco around the base of the trunk in honor of the tree's soul. These peaceful North American people, known more readily by their European name of Delaware Indians, felt that by honoring a tree in this way, its soul would be reborn by growing another tree. Telling Archie about the Leni-Lenape, I knelt down to nestle some golden grass and rotting leaves around the stump.

During the housing spurt in the post–WWII years, the trees in my neighborhood were not so honored. Rather, large machines would effortlessly doze trees into huge piles that were then set ablaze. Instead of saplings finding root, houses found their footings. While the plentiful supplies needed to build these houses provided an endless wealth of materials from which I and my friends built shacks, there were less and less woods in which to put them. The last childhood spot to yield to massive machines was a sandlot that we tagged our baseball field.

Not the athletic type, I was consistently assigned right field, deep right field, where baseballs were seldom seen. On the rare occasion when a lefty stood at bat, the more experienced and athletic outfielders moved my way, just in case. Since I didn't especially like to play baseball, deep right field was Mecca. Safe from bouncing grounders or fly balls that I always misjudged, I was able to concentrate my attention on other things. Especially drawn to the surrounding woods, I made careful note of the kinds of trees and underbrush close by. Second growth. Lots of white birch, sumac, sassafras, and aspen. Huckleberry bushes spread out at the sandy edge, creating a corridor between the sandlot and the woods. Plenty of saplings took advantage of the daylong sunny area by finding root among the short underbrush. One sapling in particular caught my eye.

The reddish satiny sheen of a yellow birch as tall as my eleven-year-old frame sat shimmering in the bright sunlight. Derivatives from this kind of birch, known as *Betula*, is used to make birch beer, a favorite of mine as a child and it remains so today. For no particular reason I became extremely attached to this tree, and its mere presence made my long trek from the dugout to deep right field more enjoyable.

One day as our scrub team walked down the woodsy path that led to the sandlot, there sat a fearsome bulldozer. We tried to pretend that all was normal, but as we chose sides, I think we shared the foreboding that today's game might well be our last. My visits to right field that day were punctuated by longer and longer visits with my young birch tree. During one of the innings, I got the idea to tie my handkerchief to the highest branch as a flag to ward off the evil dozer. The next morning, I went immediately to the sandlot to check my tree. The path was torn open to a rough, deeply treaded road. The backstop that we had fashioned of chicken wire and small tree trunks was no more. In the middle of the sandlot was a pyre, a huge pile of trees and brush awaiting kerosene and match. I wandered along the edge of what was left of the field and headed for deep right. Still standing, my dear birch tree was only inches from the threatening dozer tracks that passed by. One of its branches hung at a crude, twisted angle with its topmost edge touching the ground. A few tenacious slivers held that branch to its life-giving trunk. Its leaves were withering. I removed my handkerchief-flag from the top of the tree and used it to sling the broken branch to its trunk. Then I ran home for help.

Mrs. Gibbons, our next-door neighbor who prized and nurtured her backyard apple trees, came to the rescue with what she called her father's tree balm. I rushed back to the ailing birch, applied the balm and rewrapped the wound. The next day, I returned to visit my young patient only to find it replaced by a newly dug foundation. The distant sound of the idling Model A engine crept into my consciousness, dispersing the childhood memory like a disturbed cobweb.

Back in the present, I stood to follow Archie along a footpath that only he could see leading into the fragrant grove of hemlocks. Standing on the thick, spongy, pine needle floor of the grove, we paused in the dappled, shadowy quiet. I could see where deer slept, their bodies having compressed the needles in soft depressions. Puffs of overturned brown needles gave away their hoofprints that disappeared deeper into the grove. Archie had led me into a place of honor. My senses overwhelming any conscious thought, I stood transfixed, simply taking in the sheer beauty of the moment. I heard Archie's voice. "I'll meet you back at the Weasel, take your time."

"No, Archie," I shook myself from my mystic state. "I'll come along," I said, "otherwise, I may never leave this place."

Archie turned and I followed to make our way back to the Weasel. I noticed, to the side of the path, a small tree with a broken limb. "Archie, look at this. Should we fix it?"

"Probably a deer," Archie commented. Rather than tie a bandage around the broken branch as I did twenty-one years earlier, Archie took out his razor-sharp pocketknife and cut it off. "It's young enough to work it out," Archie said as we continued on our way.

Still having no sense of direction or bodily security, I clung to a smoothly worn spot on the grab bar, bouncing uncontrollably as the Weasel wended its way through the forest. I was surprised as the cabin came into view. Our circuitous drive through the woods brought us back to the cabin on a different road than the one we initially took into the woods.

With the Weasel, battery safely disconnected, locked into its shed, Archie and I headed home. "Your woods are striking, Archie. How many acres do you have?"

"Seven hundred and thirty-seven," Archie said, followed by an extended high-pitched, pleasure-filled laugh.

# 8 · Nature Trails

To inquire into the intricacies of a distant landscape, then, is to provoke thoughts about one's own interior landscape, and the familiar landscapes of memory. The land urges us to come around to an understanding of ourselves. . . .

There is a word from the time of the cathedrals: agape, an expression of intense spiritual affinity with the mystery that is "to be sharing life with other life." Agape is love . . . it is a humble, impassioned embrace of something outside the self. . . . We are clearly indebted . . . to the play of our intelligence . . . but we do not know whether intelligence is reason or . . . this desire to embrace and be embraced in the pattern [called] God. Whether intelligence, in other words, is love.

Barry Lopez, *Arctic Dreams*, 1986

"Well, look what the wind blew in. Are the Rocky Mountains still where they're supposed to be?" Archie greeted me, referring to my return from a month in Aspen, Colorado, where I went to study choral conducting with internationally recognized German conductor Helmuth Rilling.

"Except for the few rocks I brought back, I suppose they are. What's happening here? Any work you want me to do?" My musical side sated, I was eager to return to hands-on work.

"As a matter of fact, there is. Why don't we head up to the woods? And while we're at it, we can take the long way and drop this piece off in Prentice. Besides, it's about time you met him anyway."

"Who?" I asked, bewildered.

"Harry, the airplane mechanic that lives up in the woods. I told you about him. Anyway, I need to drop this piece of machinery off."

"Isn't that the piece I helped you weld?" I asked.

"Yup."

"What's it for anyway, Archie?"

"I made it for a fellow who fixes hydraulic hoses for lumbermen. We better get going."

Swinging open the old church doors that Archie had salvaged for his shop, he backed his truck into the large shop bay where, using his chain hoist, we loaded the awkward piece onto his truck.

We headed east on Highway 8 and an hour later, on the outskirts of Prentice, stopped by Reuban's Sales and Service, part junkyard, part anything else made of or having to do with metal.

"Hello, Archie. What brings you out this way?" Paul Bloomberg, the owner, asked.

"Dropping something off to one of your neighbors. No sense driving by without seeing what you have to offer. Mind if I walk the yard?" Archie asked.

"You go right ahead. I got a new load of stuff in, you might just want to take a look at it," Paul said, referring to a massive pile of unsorted metal fragments visible through an open bay behind his office.

"Who are you?" Paul asked me, not mincing words. "You related to Archie?"

"No, just a friend. This is some place you've got here," I said, amazed at the mixture of things cluttering what passed for an office. The walls and floor were covered with an array of new and used tools, animal hides, antique furniture, old signs, out-of-date calendars, washboards, and many objects that I had no name for.

"Well, you might as well just look around, too. Some good stuff out there. Your money's as good as anybody else's."

Joining Archie as he rummaged through the yard, I noticed an old steel bed, complete with brass fittings. Calling his attention to the bed, I asked Archie, "How much should I offer for this? It would make a great bed for Kimberly."

"Let me look around a bit. If I find anything I want, I'll deal with Paul."

Archie had picked up an unidentifiable object and we headed back to the office. "How much you want for this?" Archie asked, holding whatever it was up to Paul.

"Fifteen dollars. That's bronze."

"I know what it's made out of and it isn't worth your price. I'll give you five."

"Five?" Paul feigned deep disappointment. "Make it ten and it's yours."

"Seven and you throw in that good-for-nothing steel bed out there."

"Archie, since it's you, I'll give you both for eight dollars. That's a deal and you know it."

"Seven-fifty."

"Sold."

"Go get the bed, Deek, we better leave while we can," Archie directed.

Within minutes we were headed into town to drop off the piece Archie had made. When we pulled up to a small loading dock jutting from a small shop, however, all that greeted us was a small yellowed note that appeared to be permanently nailed to a locked door. It read, BACK IN A HOUR.

Tossing me a heavy pair of leather gloves, Archie directed me to one side of the rear of the truck, and together we slid the piece onto the dock. According to Archie there wasn't another thing to be done and so we were quickly back in the truck heading north on Route 13. After a few miles, we turned onto a seldom traveled gravel road and proceeded toward Archie's land and, as I understood, a meeting with Harry.

We slowly made our way east through dense forest and untamed land. The trip had, for some reason, put me in a contemplative mood, so I blurted out a question that had been on my mind for some time. "Archie," I asked, "do you think of your work as artistic?" He looked at me through a frowning face like he had just smelled something bad. Before he could answer, I continued, "You know, when you designed that piece we left back in Prentice, did you consider how it would look once it was in place?"

Still frowning, he cocked his head to the left and said, "What?" his face freezing in a contorted, twisted manner as he enunciated the "t."

I repeated my question adding, "When you make something from scratch, do you think of it as being more than just a functional piece?"

"Where did you put those rocks that you stole from the Rockies? In your head? Whatever I make comes out looking like what it's made for."

"Well, Archie, I mean more than that. When you make something, do you put yourself into the work—is part of you back there in that piece of steel?"

Archie's frown returned, but this time his face was pensive. "On the top of it, I suppose that you have something there. Where do you get all these notions?" he asked rhetorically, lowering the visor to keep rays of morning sun from his eyes.

"Really, Archie, this is important to me. You must have thought about what all this making things means to you. I need to know what you think about when you make something. Remember when I helped you weld this piece?" I asked. "You said that I should let myself go. Remember saying that I should let myself flow with the weld? Archie, what did you mean by that?"

Shifting in his seat he said, "Deek, I used to sharpen saws for the lumbermen. The better I sharpened, the faster they cut. The faster they cut, the more money they made. The more money they made, the more people wanted me. I was known around these parts for sharpening saws and nobody could do it better. I'd run from one camp to the next no matter what the weather, hot or cold, it didn't matter. I made good money and lots of men knew my work. I stayed over many nights in whatever camp I was in when it got dark. One night, a man named George, and I never asked or knew his last name, asked me what I was going to do when I got older. He said that I had a knack for this sort of thing and that I ought to go and learn a trade to better myself, that sharpening saws had no future."

"How old were you?" I asked.

"Younger than you are now."

"Archie, I'm thirty-two years old," I said.

"Yup, as I said, I was younger than you are now, a lot younger, twice as young."

Lillian's admonition ringing in my ears, I asked cautiously but with assurance, "What about school?"

"What good was school?" Archie retorted. "They didn't care one whip about whether I could make things. All they cared about was books. I quit in the eighth grade. We lived down in Port Arthur then, tiny place just south of town. I had no time for books." Archie's answer was emphatic but not given in anger. I turned in my seat, put my back against the door, brought my right foot up, tucking it under my left thigh, and relaxed.

Archie continued. "George was right. Staying up in the woods was okay, but I knew what he was talking about. I had been wondering what to do for some time. I went to the lumber mill to see if I could get steady work sharpening their knives and huge saw blades. You know, Deek, sharpening one of those big blades is more than just getting an edge to the teeth. Why, those blades are made to straighten out at a certain speed so they don't bind. A good sawyer could tell by the sound of the blade if it was going to bind or not. Anyway, I met a fellow who took an interest in me. He recognized my ability to fix and make things and before too long I was working at machining. It felt good, Deek, and I learned real fast that if something didn't feel right, then it wasn't. And I'll tell you, when I watched you weld that joint, it didn't feel right and it didn't look right. The way you took to it, I figured that you knew something about welding, but you weren't welding, you were proving. That's what made me say what I did." Archie fell silent.

I sat more upright. Archie was in a rare expansive mood and I felt things opening up. He seemed as willing to talk of his past as I was willing to hear it.

"When did you meet Lillian?" I asked, moving into more personal territory.

Without hesitation, Archie answered, "I was in my thirties and Lillian was twenty. She came to work at our house, to look after my mother, who was sick at the time. We went off and got married in Minneapolis. Didn't tell a soul. We just left one day, got married, and came back."

"So what did the family say, were they upset?"

"Yup, I guess they were."

Our candid discussion came to an end as we turned right onto Fedyn Road, the familiar lane leading to Archie's woods. Passing the iron gate that guarded the lane, we continued for about a quarter of a mile through an open gate at the dead end of the road. Following a grassy lane, we drove past a large mown field, around a modest raised ranch house with an attached two-stall garage and up a well-groomed dirt road. Veering to the right, we crossed a heavily built log bridge, then headed straight for a large, Quonset-style building.

"That's Harry's hangar," Archie said nonchalantly, as if an airplane hangar were a common sight in the middle of the woods. As we drove around to the front of the hangar, a huge yellow bulldozer—the kind that was used to destroy the sandlot baseball field of my youth—came into view.

Standing on top of the left, heavy steel track of a Caterpillar D7 bulldozer, a man I figured was Harry grabbed the vertical crank that stuck oddly through the top of the engine cover and gave it a hard, quick twist. A light cough, and sputter followed.

"Hi, Harry," Archie yelled up to the man. Harry just waved his hand behind his back, crouched down on top of the steel tread of the dozer, and peered into the rear of the engine compartment. "You should let me fix that overgrown kitten of yours, then maybe it'll do some work for you," Archie called up sarcastically. Harry's response was a muffled, indiscernible mixture of shortened vowels and emphatic consonants.

Pulling his head from the engine compartment, Harry twisted the crank once again and brought a small, two-cylinder gas starter engine to life. The Caterpillar D7's main engine, a hefty four-cylinder diesel, often overwhelmed its electric starter, so a pony engine was used to get the thing going. Harry engaged the pinion that connected the pony engine to the diesel. With the big engine in full decompression, he then engaged the pony engine's clutch lever, and the reluctant diesel began turning over. Under its heavy load, the pony engine nearly stalled, but by deftly working the clutch, Harry was able to keep its two cylinders popping. Reaching farther into the rear of the engine compartment, Harry pulled the decompression lever to its halfway position, then once again engaged the pony engine clutch. The beastly diesel responded with a bone-jangling bang and belched a cloud of dark smoke from its vertical exhaust pipe. Reaching for a can of compressed ether, Harry spurted some of the liquid into the intake manifold. Almost instantly, a few more bangs came from the big engine along with black, stinking exhaust. A few more spurts of ether and the big engine kicked in, its roaring sound obliterating the now fast-running pony engine. Turning off the smaller engine, Harry yelled loudly to Archie, "Check the gauges!" Archie crawled up to the cab of the bulldozer and, crouching down on the padded seat, peered under the overhanging engine cover.

Seeing that the fuel and oil pressure gauge needles were in the green, Archie gave Harry the thumbs-up sign, left his high perch in the cab of the Cat, and stood again by my side. Harry walked a few steps from along the steel tracks and flopped onto the seat. Pulling on a few levers that set the behemoth in motion, Harry looked down at me and nodded his head, making no attempt to say anything over the roar of the Cat, and headed the machine toward his 3,600-foot airfield.

"Archie," I said as the noise of the bulldozer faded in the distance, "I thought you brought me up here to meet Harry. Was that it?"

"Yup. Besides, there will be other times. When Harry's fooling around with that Cat of his, it's no time to visit. Might as well talk to a tree. I guess he has to fix something on the landing strip."

"Now that raises another question, Archie. Why does Harry have an airfield in the middle of the woods?"

"Because if you're going to work on planes, you need a place to land and take off."

"Obviously, but why here? Why not use the airport?"

"Harry wanted his own. He and I have been friends for years. During the war, number two that is, Harry went to California to build planes and that's where he stayed until he came back here in the sixties. He bought the land, built an airstrip and a few buildings, and that was that. People know Harry, so they bring their planes here to be worked on. Harry owns four hundred and fifty-nine acres up here. They mix and match with my two hundred and seventy-five, so together we own over a square mile of woods."

Without a map, there was no telling where Archie's land ended and Harry's began. They had a gentleman's agreement: What was Archie's was Harry's and what was Harry's was Archie's. To those who knew Archie, the acreage was referred to as Archie's woods. Conversely, Harry's friends referred to them as Harry's woods. For me, it was Archie's woods.

"What do you do with it all, why so much land?" I asked earnestly.

"Why not? Deek, I just don't understand you sometimes. It's a place to come to. With land like this there's no place else I need to go. Besides, somebody has to own it. Isn't that the way of it? Do you know any land that isn't owned by somebody? You won't find it. Harry and I take it seriously, Deek. We'd rather be here doing for the creatures than having somebody wrecking the place. It's a matter of responsibility. Does that answer your question?"

"Archie, do we have time for you to give me a tour?"

"Let's go get the Weasel," Archie said with a boyish glint in his eye.

Soon we were chugging our way through densely forested trails in the wonderful Weasel, my sense of direction being somewhat like that of a pilot in a snowstorm. But it didn't matter; I wasn't lost, just transported. Compared to my first visit when trees and brush were in early bloom, the woods was lush and thick. The air was close. Waves seemed to float off the dark green, fully leaved branches of surrounding trees, reminding me of a Charles Burchfield watercolor. Crickets and creatures of the underbrush chirped and rustled, their sounds amplifying the heat of August.

The Weasel soon took us to the hemlock grove, where Archie stopped. "Remember that, Deek?" Archie said, pointing to the area where we visited the cherry tree stump. I nodded, having already recognized the sacred spot. I was feeling serene—Archie's woods once again drew me in with its power and majesty.

As we bounced along, Archie commented, "Look for the moss on the trees. It always grows on the north side. You might need to know that someday."

According to the moss on the tree bark, we were heading north, the familiar hemlock grove being to our right. Coming to a crossroad, we took a right turn for a short distance, then again headed north on a wide, grass-covered lane. "We're on Grass Road. Years ago, it used to be a lumber road, but Harry cleaned it up and planted grass," Archie informed me. At the turn of the century, Grass Road was a main trunk for hauling lumber out of the dense woods. It ran a distance of a mile and a quarter south from Harry's airplane hangar to the northernmost part of their land, which was capped by the Thornapple River.

Making a right turn off Grass Road, the Weasel took us down a very narrow, twisting trail to the edge of a large beaver pond. Archie turned off the ignition and we sat in the still, quiet peace of raw nature. Within a few moments, I heard the sound of working beavers—slapping tails and rustling water. Leaving the Weasel, we took a short walk along the edge of the pond. The spongy ground sank underfoot. Water rose halfway up my shoes. Archie pointed out the cone shapes of beaver-cut tree stumps. The dammed water of Spring Creek had spread out, submerging undergrowth and the bottoms of trees. Drowned, dead trees, some standing, others strewn about like just-dropped pick-up-sticks, presented a macabre scene—gray death contrasting with the placid sight of the reflective pond. "They mate for life, you know," Archie informed me. "Smart creatures. Lots to learn from them, Deek." When we returned to the Weasel, Archie retrieved a small bow saw from under the Weasel's seat and cut a piece from one of the beaver cuttings. "Here, take this to those kids of yours. I bet they never saw a beaver cutting before." This was not country-lane type land or tame suburban woods. This was wild and tough, filled with animals going about their business and plants competing for nourishment and sunlight. I began to understand Archie's comment about owning the land out of a sense of responsibility, and I was awed by it.

Seated back in the Weasel, we headed north on the muddy road. The big, chain-covered wheels splattered sticky mud along the back of my right arm and shoulder. Coming to another stand of hemlocks, Archie pointed to a hill. "That's Wolf Hill. Lots of wolves up here. It's 1,273 feet above sea level, the highest spot in my woods."

We circled back to Grass Road then headed north to what Archie referred to as Boat Landing, a small, sandy ramp that led to the Thornapple's watery edge. "From here, the Thornapple twists around for a mile and a half before reaching my cabin. Starts twenty-five miles north of here, up in the Chequamegon National Forest. Lots of smart old bass, pike, muskie, trout, and river beavers call this home. Do you fish?" Archie asked.

I told Archie of my childhood days when my grandfather took me fishing at his serene fishing club near the Pocono Mountains. It had become a custom to go fishing with Grandpa early on summer Saturday mornings, returning home before noon, having some lunch, then going down to his basement shop to work. An avid fly fisherman, Grandpa had thousands of flies and lures. all sorts of bamboo rods, tackle, small weighing devices, and rulers to help keep him legal and honest; lead weights, leader (some as fine as baby hair), and tiny tools capable of tying the tiniest fly to the thinnest leader.

Looking at the tumbling clear Thornapple, I imagined that my grandfather would have done just about anything to fish these waters, so in his memory I asked Archie if I could fish the river. He gave me permission to fish and added hunting for good measure, providing that I would take the time to learn the lay of the land. He didn't want me getting lost. I relished the assignment.

With the Weasel parked at Boat Landing, we walked along River Road, which ran along the south bank of the Thornapple. Suddenly, Archie's left arm arced upward with his strong open-palmed hand toward me. It was the kind of gesture a school crossing guard might use to keep back a rambunctious child. "Do you see it?" I looked around me, seeing nothing but the rough beauty of trees and underbrush to my left, the grassy path in front of me, and the Thornapple to my right. I shook my head. I didn't see anything.

His left arm moved from in front of me, his open hand now forming a pointing gesture. I followed his arm's line until my eyes caught the form of a gray wolf, whose color flowed into the shadowy underbrush. This wolf was not the majestic creature given to us in wildlife magazines. It had a scraggly pelt and a lean torso, more like a stray dog than king of the hill; yet, there it was. The first wolf I had ever seen in the wild, and I stood motionless. After a few minutes of reverence, Archie signaled us on our way. As we walked farther along the path, the wolf kept a respectful distance, paralleling our walk while keeping a wary eye on our movements. Like a bird in the sky that gets lost in the clouds, the wolf eventually melded into the woods, disappearing from sight.

"You know, Deek, some people would just as well shoot that creature as take a breath. Now, you asked before about me and Harry having all this land, well, now you know. That wolf is safe here as long as we have anything to do about it."

Archie and Harry kept a close eye on their woods. They kept the trails groomed and always made sure that the creatures were protected from poachers or reckless hunters. I never broached the subject with Archie, but from what I heard from townspeople, trespassers got rough treatment. Because Archie and Harry were careful of who they invited to hunt, it was an honor for those who received permission.

On our way back to the Weasel, Archie asked, "Do you have a gun?"

I told Archie that I had three guns, which piqued his curiosity.

"What kind are they?"

"A Remington twelve-gauge over-and-under, an Ansley Fox, and a thirty-five Remington."

"You want to sell them? I'll give you a good price for the Fox."

"No, I don't want to sell them. Why do you want to buy them?"

He never answered, just looked at me and prodded a bit about selling the guns. It was only when I emphatically told him I wasn't selling that he relaxed with a promise to show me his collection.

As we continued on our journey through the woods, Archie carefully pointed out various landmarks so that I might find my way whenever I was alone in the woods. One such landmark was a rough shelter that Archie called a creature blind. He and Harry had a number of these camouflaged lean-tos throughout the woods, where they would go to watch nature. They made good stand posts during deer hunting season as well, Archie was quick to inform me.

Heading south on Grass Road, Archie pointed out a small area that appeared to be impenetrable. "Tag alders," he commented. "A good place for deer to hide. Those other trees are tamaracks. Some people call them larch. When these woods were timbered out, they used those trees for railroad ties, posts, and everything in between. Ever been over a corduroy road? They used to lay tamarack down over the wetlands. Lots around these parts. Lose your teeth going over one."

Clearly in his element, I sat quietly enjoying Archie's monologue on the joys of nature. He told me about hardwood and soft wood, the ways of quail, how to find hibernating bear in the dead of winter, why wolves howl, plus a whole lot of other facts that just melded into the pleasure of the afternoon.

Past the tag alder swamp, we turned abruptly east to avoid driving into the meandering Thornapple then south toward the cabin, which we approached from yet a different direction than we had the previous week. It was three-thirty in the afternoon. We had driven around Archie's woods for a bit over five and a half hours. With the exception of Grass Road, we had not retraced our way on any of the trails.

Including the mile-long Grass Road, seventeen miles of nature trails wove their way through Archie's woods. While Harry neatly put roads around each of his forty-acre tracts, Archie's trails wandered here and there with no apparent rhyme or reason. "How did you decide where to put your roads?" I asked as we stopped by the cabin.

"Well, the way I see it, if anyone gets on them that doesn't belong on them, he'll walk in circles till I catch him," Archie laughed. Then in a more serious tone, he said, "Years ago, they cut the trees out of here without a care. When I put these roads in, I didn't cut down one tree that otherwise wouldn't have fallen over or been ruined by bigger trees. Harry, his son Dick, and I spent a few years laying out these roads. Why, we surveyed every stitch of it, went around every forty. No sense to be cutting down the forest if you don't need to."

Clearly, Archie pronounced Dick as *Dick*, not *Deek*, as he called me.

"Archie, you call Harry's son Dick and me Deek. Did you know that?"

"Of course I know that. You're Deek and Dick is Dick. You're two different people, so why not have two different names," he said with a chuckle.

"We do, Archie. I mean, I introduced myself to you as Richard. Remember?"

"That was months ago. You never said anything about it. Why didn't you say something if it bothered you so much?" Archie asked, his voice rising.

"It doesn't bother me. If it did, I would have said something, you can be sure of that."

"Does it bother you now?"

"No, Archie, it doesn't."

"Well, now you really have me confused. If you don't mind me calling you Deek then why are we talking about this?"

"I'm curious, Archie, probably just trying to figure you out. You know you're very complex and smart as hell?"

Archie ignored my question and pulled the Weasel up to its stall. Repeating his comment about the creatures gnawing cables, Archie disconnected the battery and locked up. "No sense going back empty." Archie directed my attention to a large pile of cut and split firewood. "Let's load up the truck." With the back piled with wood, we drove back to town on the now familiar County J. Instead of stopping at his place, we headed directly to the Indianhead.

This time when the locals greeted Archie, he said to them, "Well, boys"—nudging the calf of my leg as a cue to go along— "we saw a white wolf today, as big as any I've ever seen." The boys became agitated. Archie went on to lie in detail about how he and I came across this rare find, pinpointing a location some twenty miles from his land. Eyes got as big as saucers. The men talked as if Archie had seen a god, and before we left the Indianhead, they were swapping stories, one bigger than the next.

"What was that all about, Archie?" I asked, as we headed back to his house.

"Deek, those boys don't ever have much to say, you know that. The white wolf will keep them busy for a long time. You know, don't be too hard on them. They're a good lot even though they're as lazy as it gets. You know they have the same vote you do, or have you forgot?"

"A little scary, isn't it Archie?"

"Not one bit. Now, not everybody is as educated as you are. Some folks vote from what they think and feel. That's the way it should be."

He seemed to be challenging me, and I was about to bite when we reached Archie's house. The conversation ended. We unloaded the wood into a now empty drying shed.

"Where's all the wood that was here?" I asked.

"In the basement. I can hardly burn wood out here, it won't do a lick of good."

"You have a wood-burning furnace?"

"Yup, backed up with gas just in case I need to go away for a few days. It used to be that in the winter, one stayed put or the fire went out. That's changed. You want to see it? Come on."

"By the looks of things, you boys put in a good day," Lillian said, as we entered the house. "Did you enjoy the woods?"

"The woods are wonderful." Looking at Archie, I continued, "Lillian, we saw a white wolf. According to Archie, here, it was a rare find."

"You did," she responded with feigned motherly surprise. "A white wolf is rare all right."

Smiling like a young boy caught in a ruse, Archie headed for the basement. "Follow me."

Sure enough, Archie had two furnaces, one gas-fired, the other wood. But Archie had more in mind than showing me his heating system. Along one wall that ran two-thirds the length of his house, Archie had installed a gun rack. "Over a hundred guns there," he said proudly. "You sure you don't want those shotguns of yours added to the collection?" I didn't answer. "Got others, too, but I keep them hidden away. I might show you someday." His comment was laced with intrigue. Archie proceeded down his row of guns, now and then stopping to point out a special piece in his collection.

Below the rack were shelves covered with numerous objects, including a collection of arrowheads, knives, some antique tools, numerous rocks, some cut in half to display insides full of crystals. Tucked in the far corner of the shelf where it met the opposing wall was a short row of old, leather-bound books. Seeing my surprise, Archie offered, "Old engine books, Deek." Reaching for a small, pocket-size black leather-bound book, he asked, "Know anything about steam?"

"Not very much."

"Well, take this along. You might learn something," Archie said, handing me *Roper's Catechism of Steam Engines*.

# 9 · Baptism

*There is always one moment in childhood
when the door opens and lets the future in.*

Graham Greene, *The Power and the Glory*, 1940

I walked into the shop with my son, Jason, to find Archie leaning over the mechanical hacksaw with his back to the door.

"Good morning, Deek," Archie said without looking up from his work. When I asked what he was doing, he made a show of exasperation and replied, "I'm making a part for my winch. I bought a new truck and need to refit a coupling. They're always changing things that don't need it."

My guess was that he was enjoying the challenge as he always seemed to do when he improved on someone else's design. Archie bought a new truck every two years, always a three-quarter-ton Chevy with a standard transmission and no frills. Just as he did with his shop machinery, he altered his truck to suit his needs, which in this case meant installing a winch of his own design and manufacture made from two Model A Ford transmissions linked in tandem. The winch was every bit as powerful as any found on a sizable tow truck. In its design, the winch was hidden from view so that no one looking at the truck would know it was there. Archie kept the winch hidden, like an ace up his sleeve; with the exception of using it to slide heavy machinery onto his trailer, he used it only when he could step into a situation and come out a hero.

"Well," Archie said as he turned to see me and Jason standing in the open doorway, "look what the cat brought in."

Normally, Archie would have returned to his work dragging me, most likely, into his project. But seeing Jason, he set his work aside and came over to where we were standing.

Before Archie reached us, Jason pointed to a stack of steel stock, asking "What that?"

"That's steel," Archie answered matter-of-factly.

"What that?" Jason asked, keeping up his assault.

Looking at me, Archie said, "The apple doesn't fall far from the tree, that's for sure. Too many questions."

I leapt in, explaining that steel was used to make things, which seemed to satisfy Jason. Archie was off the hook.

Still focused on me, Archie said, referring to the pile of steel stock, "Well, I guess as long as you're here you might as well help me rack these few pieces." I knew that Archie wasn't ignoring Jason, just a bit uncomfortable. With Jason watching, I spent a few minutes with Archie racking the steel. When we finished, I reached down and picked up a small piece of round stock about the size of a fat pencil. "No reason why Jason can't join in," I said to Archie.

"Nope, don't suppose there is, but you better let me clean up the edges, they're pretty sharp, you know." I handed the small piece of steel to Archie.

"Well," Archie said looking down at Jason, "I think that you better take this daddy of yours outside while I grind this. I don't want to scare him," he said jokingly, referring to my dislike of the dreadful grinder.

Five minutes later, Archie joined us in the clear sunshine. The small piece of stock was ground smooth with a lustre that could only come from being carefully wire brushed. It was a small enough gesture, to be sure, but by the look of things it wasn't only the steel's edges that were eased. This was something new for Archie. On the few previous occasions that I brought Jason to the shop, Archie was friendly enough, but remote, as if Jason's youth was, in and by itself, intimidating. This was different.

Archie bent down to Jason's level and handed him the warm steel. Jason shot a beam of delight my way. "Well, what do you say, Jason?"

"Tank oo," he said to Archie in a small voice.

"You're welcome," Archie said quietly and walked back into his shop.

In a flash, Jason plopped down with his new tool and busied himself digging away in the sandy soil where the driveway met the lawn. Leaving Jason to enjoy himself, I returned to the shop, where for ten minutes or so Archie and I worked together on his truck. When I went to check on Jason, he was covered with dirt.

"What are you up to?" I asked Jason as I walked up to him.

"Dirty," he said, holding out his left hand with palm up.

"Why?"

"Like you."

"What?" I asked, surprised.

"Like Ouchy," he said, meaning Archie.

"You mean that you want to work and get real dirty doing it?" I taunted with widening eyes.

Instantaneously, Jason was immersed in a cloud of dust, the permission to get dirtier taken on with purpose, delight, joy, and all of the stuff that boys are made of.

I took his "like you" to heart—the little shaver, the chip off the old block. Was my son telling me that he wanted to work with machinery and get all oily and dirty? Hmmm? Did Jason want to get little slivers of hot steel cut into his hands? Did he want his fingernails to never be clean again and tough calluses sprouting on his palms? How about some scars to remind him of a few slipups and blackened cracks on the outside of his index finger to make it as rough as eighty-grit sandpaper? Did he want his palm creases, those lines that fortunetellers read, packed full of minute particles of dirt? Did he want to pick out splinters with the tip of a super-sharp penknife? Was Jason saying that he wanted to wrap his hand around the tote of a plane or the handle of a chisel? Did he want to sharpen a blade so fine that it could cut the hair off your arm? Was Jason saying that he appreciated the fine and noble feeling of making things with your hands?

Of course not. I was telling myself that, kicking back to Grandpa and my early days. But Jason was imitating what Archie and I did, and that was enough for me.

Jason stood from his squatting position at the edge of the driveway, displaying the small palms of his soil-stained hands like badges of courage.

"Well, come on Jason, it's time to wash up."

Jason followed me into Archie's shop, where just to the left of the door, the sawed-off wooden whiskey barrel filled with gray water beckoned. Archie joined us at the barrel and offered to Jason's eager reach the can of Crisco-like hand cleaner that sat near the washtub. Jason proudly dipped his dirty hands into the soft mixture and rubbed the slippery cleaner between his hands with tiny, uncertain circles. When Archie and I bent over to rinse our hands in the cool water, Jason reached up to do the same. "Here, Jason," Archie said, as he slid a thick block of wood over to the barrel. "Step on this." The three of us stood around the barrel rinsing, Jason imitating Archie and I as we pulled the water up to our wrists with cupped hands. I liken the moment to a baptism through which my son was officially joined to the sacred world of working men.

After drying our hands on harsh brown paper towels, Jason and I stepped out of Archie's shop and into the bright Saturday morning light. Archie followed, locking up.

"Let me see those hands of yours," Archie directed Jason.

Jason turned his palms upward. Archie bent down and took Jason's tiny fingers in his hand for a careful inspection. "Yup," he said as he stood, giving a nod of approval verified with pursed lips. "You've got good hands," he complimented Jason.

The human hand is, perhaps, the greatest machine ever fashioned by Mother Nature. To be certain it stays warm, she put fifteen feet of blood vessels and capillaries to every square inch of hand. I guessed that the veins in Archie's hands could run the length of four football fields. For hard work, she gave the hand its own glove factory in the form of horny cells that can pile up to four millimeters thick. Imagine having calluses as thick as a thin pamphlet. So that we can grab, hold, and manipulate, she put in twenty-seven bones, each carefully connected with cartilage, tendons, and muscles. And just so things don't slip, she gave the fingertips little ridges on one side, and to protect the tips, fingernails on the other. Now for the amazing part. To make sure that we stay in touch with ourselves, she gave them feeling. Millions of nerve endings sending quick signals to the brain for instant analysis.

When Archie extended his hand to Jason, I thought about the wonder of it all. Jason's baby-fat hands full of potential, Archie's full of knowledge and skill. Too bad all that skill just didn't travel right through Archie's nerve endings to Jason's. If Jason wanted it, he would just have to get it himself. Mother Nature doesn't give experience, just potential.

"Well, I'll see you boys some other time. Lillian and I have a date with nature. One of these days, you have to bring that family of yours up to see my woods."

As Archie walked away I turned to Jason and asked if he wanted to go to the Indianhead.

"What that?" he asked.

"A place to buy you some chocolate milk."

"Why?"

"Because I want a cup of coffee. Would you like a glass of chocolate milk?"

As I suspected, he couldn't turn down the opportunity to get his favorite drink.

I wasn't being entirely truthful with Jason. I had an ulterior
motive. Like many boys whose early years were spent surrounded by the happenings of World War II, I was enamored of Jeeps.
My ride in Archie's Weasel rekindled my childhood love affair
and I had made up my mind to find one. I planned to restore it,
plow snow with it, and maybe even drive through Archie's
woods with it. I had yet to discuss the idea with Archie, but
planned to bring it up as time went on. But first things first. I
had to find a Jeep, model CJ2A, a civilian adaptation of the real
thing.

I had learned from Archie that the boys at the Indianhead,
while not in the least interested in talking, had their hands on
who was doing what, what was for sale, who was moving, what
jobs were opening up, and usually accurate weather forecasts. I
figured if anyone would know where I might find one, it was one
of them.

As I entered the cafe with Jason, the usual eyes looked up, but
being a stranger, I was not welcomed as was Archie; rather, I was
greeted by silence. I ordered a cup of coffee for myself and a glass
of chocolate milk for Jason. As we sat in the gloomy silence of
the Indianhead, I looked across to the opposing counter and
asked, "Does anyone know where I might find an old Jeep?"

The men looked up in a quiet stare broken by one fellow who
asked, "What for?"

"I'm interested in finding an old Jeep to fix up. Do any of you
know where I might find one?" I answered, not sure what he
meant by "what for."

The men huddled close to one another and spoke in low tones.

"You the guy that was with Archie when he saw the white
wolf?" asked the same fellow who had asked "what for."

"That's me," I answered directly. The men returned to their huddle.

"Well hey, was Archie pullin' our leg?" another asked. "Sometimes he does that, you know. Hey, with Archie, a person never knows. He's good at it, too, that's for sure. Isn't he?" he asked the other men, who nodded or grunted an affirmative.

Supporting Archie's innocent ruse, I assured the men that we had seen a white wolf. "I didn't see it at first," I offered, "but Archie pointed it out to me."

"Oh yeah, that's Archie. Why, he can see things nobody else does. Oh, that's for sure," said a fellow who was sitting at the end of the pack. I interpreted his comment as sarcasm until he continued, "You know, that Archie, whys he's got those eyes that can see way beyond . . ." The man's voice ended as if he were going to conclude with another few words, but nothing more was said. Once again, the other men grunted and nodded their approval.

I repeated my request that I was looking for a Jeep.

After a few mumbles from their huddle a man said, "I heard there was one out to Jerry's place, over there west on Twenty-seven. I don't know that he would be selling it, thoughs, you have to ask him, 'cause I don't know anything about that."

When Jason and I finished, I wrestled what directions I could out of the men, thanked them, and left the Indianhead in pursuit of Jerry's place and hopefully a Jeep. After getting lost and asking for help at a mobile home sales office, Jason and I found Jerry Bradshaw's place. Sure enough, there was a Jeep and Jerry was selling. We haggled over the price a bit but I was soon the proud owner of a 1947 Willys CJ2A Jeep with no top, ragged seats, half flat and all bald tires, and a small tree growing happily in the corner by the tailgate for $125. Jerry was up on his knowledge of Jeeps and he assured me that my new purchase would do all I asked.

Within an hour, I had the Jeep towed to Marv's gas station with instructions to "Get her running, change the oil, and adjust the clutch. I'll take care of the rest."

Jason and I headed home, where before day's end, I got a call from Marv's.

"The Jeep's running, when can you pick it up? Oh, by the way, I had to fix the generator, it wasn't putting out any juice, and, of course, I put a new battery in it, six-volt—did you know that? And we decided to drain the transfer case, there was a lot of water in there, lucky it didn't freeze up and crack the case. What are you planning to do with the lights?" The man from Marv's would have continued on and on had I not interrupted.

"All I want is for the thing to be running. How much do I owe you?" I asked, knowing that it would probably be far more than I expected.

"Well, I'm glad you asked. You know I don't want anything leaving my garage that's going to break down just a few feet away so I put some extra time in it. Especially the brakes. They were real bad and needed an entire cleaning. I fixed the master cylinder. It was leaking real bad, could hardly get any pedal. And the distributor cap was cracked—I put on an old one I had lying around, but I had to put new plugs and plug wires on."

"How much?" I interrupted.

"Well, like I was saying—"

"How much? How much money do I owe you?" I asked directly.

"You mean labor and parts? I had to put a lot of parts in this. Fan belt was all but broken, but the radiator seems to hold water.

I didn't put any antifreeze in it, but you better do that with winter coming."

"Everything. How much is the total bill?—parts, labor, and towing."

"Oh, I decided to throw the towing in for free. Give me a moment to add up the bill. Hold on now."

I waited, seeing dollar signs flick by.

"Well, it looks like you owe me, not including the towing, of course, which I said that I would throw in free, a total of $75.85."

I expressed my relief with a classic "Phew!"

"Too much?" I heard at the other end of the phone. "I did a lot of work, but if it's too much, why maybe we can settle on something better."

"No," I said. "That's fine. I'll be right over."

I walked the mile or so to pick up my Jeep, paid the bill, received a warning that the gas tank probably needed to be replaced and was told, "Now don't go very far—I put air in the tires but it's not going to stay there." When he finished I gave him my thanks, started her, and pulled out of the garage proudly behind the wheel of my own Jeep with its windshield folded down on its hood. Heading down the road was a childhood dream fulfilled. I pulled it into the garage, where I let the noisy four-cylinder, flathead engine idle a bit before shutting it down.

I stood up in the Jeep like MacArthur did on his return to the Philippines. I saw Eisenhower driving Walter Cronkite along the beaches of Normandy. Scenes from *The Bridge on the River Kwai, Stalag 17,* and *MovieTone News* flicked by. Pushing the mechanical floor starter, I brought the engine back to life and gunned it just to hear the whir of the oversized fan. The sound of a Jeep was to power as the sound of a Model A was to sweetness.

My first ride in a Jeep was through the courtesy of a gardener of one of our neighbors. I was five years old and nicknamed him Jeep Man. Whenever I heard the sound of the small engine-powered reel mower come to life, I hightailed it over to my neighbor's yard, where Jeep Man was always ready to give me a ride.

When Hurricane Agnes brought its fury with silt-ridden water to Wilkes-Barre in 1972, it was a Jeep that saved the day. George Strimmel, a good friend, didn't hesitate to offer me his, which I used to transport water pumps, electric generators, tools, and volunteers through the slippery ooze and mud to the front door of my water-soaked home. It was George's Jeep that pulled my ruined Steinway out the front door, down the steps and to the curb where an army front loader and truck dispatched it to a landfill.

Now, a bit more than a year later, I had my own Jeep ready for a full renovation, for renewal, for a transformation that would bring its 1947 prowess into the 1970s. The Jeep would take me to work when snow was three-feet deep, it would plow my driveway and safely transport my family, it would pull out tree stumps, and hopefully take me into the northern Wisconsin wilds.

As I savored all of the possibilities of having a Jeep, the most exciting prospect was having access to Archie's woods—Beaver Pond at six o'clock in the morning, the Thornapple River, where wild bass lunkers waited for my bait, Wolf Hill for thinking through things, and the cherry tree stump for spiritual renewal. But first things first: I needed to get Archie involved.

# 10 · Restoring

*You cannot just talk to the stars or the silence of the night. You have to fancy some listener, or, better yet, to know of somebody whose mere existence stimulates you to talk and lends wings to your thoughts, whose nature sets a measure to your understanding. . . .*

Heinrich Zimmer, referring to a meeting with
Dr. C. G. Jung, 1932

I'm not a very good mechanic. I had never overhauled an engine or taken on the chore of restoring a car as I did the Wilkes-Barre house. Cars were something I kept running not out of honor, but rather, out of necessity. I could track my life by listing the cars I had driven, from a prewar Plymouth to the 1972 Volvo that now kept my family safe and happy. In between, in order of appearance, were a

1949 Ford flathead V8 that had a great sound; a 1950 Pontiac with an automatic transmission that, on a good day, got eight miles a gallon; a 1953 Chevy that burned oil in equal proportion to gas; a 1948 Indian Motorcycle (an aberration that cost me fifty dollars) with a suicide clutch, fender skirts, and a sound to die for, which probably many did; a 1953 Mercury V8 hardtop convertible that ate generator bearings like popcorn; a 1959 Chevy Biscayne with gull-wing rear fenders that took me to and from Pennsylvania to Indiana and through graduate school, all the while with valve lifters that collapsed without warning. In celebration of my first teaching job, I bought a 1963 Volvo 122 S that carried me and my starter family well over 150,000 miles with nary a complaint and that led to the current one complete with leather seats and an eight-track tape player.

The idea of restoring the Jeep was daunting, and I wasn't all that happy with the idea of smelly grease and flakes of rust finding their way into my ears, eyes, nose, and throat. Access to Archie's shop took on new meaning—I pictured us working long into the night bringing my Jeep to storeroom condition. Knowing that Archie was not easily brought into someone else's project, I decided that the best course of action was to show him the Jeep and slowly bring up the subject—and that Archie, being sensitive to the responsibility of properly restoring machines, would welcome the project. Or so I thought.

The next day I drove over and quickly knew that things were not going smoothly. Archie was curt, and after giving the Jeep a quick look, he asked, "What kind of tires are you going to put on this thing?" Before I could reply, Archie snarled, "You paid too much for it. That's what you paid—too much! Running to the Indianhead for advice. Serves you right."

"The boys at the Indianhead filled you in, I see. How do you know what I paid? There was no way for those guys to know that."

"Deek, when any damn fool college teacher comes to town and buys a broken down good-for-nothing Jeep for too much money, the word goes out—far beyond the Indianhead."

Instantly, my anger over Archie's sarcastic tone wedged its way through any rational response. "Bullshit, Archie. Here you go again, just like you did that night I came down when you were fixing the doorknob. What the hell do you know about what it has taken me to earn my degrees? And what the hell does this have to do with my buying a Jeep? I bought the Jeep because I want a Jeep. You can tell your informants or anybody else in this town that they can go piss up a rope."

Archie stood as if hit. He turned and walked away. I did the same by heading out the door toward my Jeep.

"Deek," I heard Archie call in a strong voice. "You never answered my question. What kind of tires are you going to put on that thing, that Jeep of yours?"

"Army issue if I can find them," I answered forthrightly without turning around.

Keeping our distance, Archie said angrily, "If you think that you're going to rope me into helping you fix that Jeep of yours, you have another thing coming. I don't want anything to do with it. That's all there is to it."

Turning and raising my hands to shoulder height with palms facing Archie, I said in a passive tone, "Hey, Archie, I'm not asking. I can do my own work, which I need to get to." I said my good-bye and turned once again toward my Jeep.

"Those army tires don't have much traction, Deek," he called after me in a gentler tone. "They're not good in the snow."

I stopped by the Jeep. There was too much at stake here. Archie had become a friend, and I admired him as much as anyone in my life. What purpose would it possibly serve for me to leave? I returned to where Archie stood, next to the open door to his shop. It was time to clear the air. Stopping about three feet from where he stood, I asked earnestly, "What's this all about, Archie? I came down here to tell you about the Jeep and I wish that you would join me in doing a restoration. I'm not ashamed to admit when I need some help."

"Well, Deek, since you asked, I will help you, but you have to do most of the work. But I think—"

"Look, Archie, this is no good. I need to know what bothers you so much about my being a teacher. I put every bit as much work into getting my degrees as you did into becoming a machinist. I'd like to get this business between us aside so we can get on with our lives."

Archie was hunched over, as if he was ready to attack, but clearly something came over him. He pursed his lips and said, "Come into the shop, there's something you need to know."

I followed Archie into the coolness of his gray shop, down the aisle past the familiar lathes and miller to the workbench by the back door. "You sit there," Archie said, motioning to a four-legged, wooden stool beefed up with twisted wire supports. As I sat, Archie pulled up a sturdy library chair with the golden hue of quartered oak still visible through cracks in its blackened, greasy patina.

Looking me straight in the eye, Archie said without any introduction or apologetic lead, "Plain and simple, Deek, I can't read. Words just don't make any sense to me when they're next to each other. Now, numbers—why, that's different. It's words that bother me. I told you from the beginning that I had no time for teachers, they and all their reading. I quit school because of it. They didn't care if I could make and fix things, or work numbers. All they cared about were words. If you couldn't read, that's all there was to it."

"Is that why you were so mad that night when you were working on the doorknob? I had never seen you so mad."

"Angry, Deek, the word is angry, only dogs get mad and you know what they do to mad dogs," he said, jokingly.

I stood up from the stool and walked a step or two out of the yellow cone cast from the porcelain-shaded overhead lamp and looked into the still, muted shadows of the shop. My eye caught some peeling paint on the side of his nut and bolt bins. How long ago, I thought, did he paint that? The huge boring mill cast an eerie, undefined shadow, a cast-iron dinosaur. The old refrigerator, where he kept his welding rods, no longer looked out of place. I saw machinery neatly arranged as if they were the innards of a living organism, each feeding the other, all dependent upon Archie to keep them running in concert. This shop and its machinery, its dusky light and smells of work was Archie. It was his classroom, studio, university, library, operating room, concert hall, and gallery. He breathed life into cold steel in this place. He cut deals and invented. I was humbled.

I turned, wanting more than anything else to question him about where he learned all that he knew about measurement, steel, machining, ratios, wood, and animals, building houses and furniture. But I held back. Did it really matter? I asked myself.

"Archie, I don't know what to say." I walked back to the stool and sat down. Archie was smiling, which caught me by surprise. I had never seen Archie smile before. His face was either somber or grinning but never smiling. I smiled back, feeling, perhaps for the first time in my life, the passion and trust that come from deep friendship.

"Here, Deek," Archie said quietly, "take a look at these." I reached out to take a rumpled stack of papers.

I leafed through the pieces of cardboard, odd-shaped remains of paper bags, and some lined notebook paper jammed together with other bits of paper of unknown origin. I leaned forward into the light to get a better look. I saw lines that looked like stick figures, scribbling, and curlicues. Abstract drawings, one page or scrap, after another, each having numbers I recognized and symbols I didn't.

"They're my drawings," Archie offered without my having asked. "They're drawings of machinery that keeps a lot of places around here in business. Some are machines I made for the sash and door company. The one you're looking at, that's a machine I made for Lillian's sister, Alma, and her husband, Walter. No one has ever seen them all together before."

My mind felt flattened, like an ill-tuned note. I was holding trust—Archie's trust—and I was overwhelmed. Their creator was sitting right across from me, and I wanted to hug him but knew better.

"You see that wagon up there," Archie directed my eyes to a model of a Conestoga wagon about the size of a lunch box that sat on a shelf above the bench. "That's what the machine I made for Alma and Walter makes. Here," he said, reaching for the wagon, "take it home to that boy of yours. If you pull the wagon tongue, a light goes on," he added gleefully.

I set the sacred sheaf of papers on the bench top and took the wagon from him with both hands. "Thank you, Archie, Jason will treasure it." I sat the wagon on my lap where I coddled it with my right hand against its side. I wished I had something to give him in return but I didn't.

The corner of Archie's machine shop had become intimate. We sat quietly until silence made us both a tad uneasy.

"Archie, do you mind if I ask you a question?"

"Well, that never stopped you before. What?"

"How did you learn all the things that you've learned without being able to read?" I guess that after all it did matter.

"That's a fair question, Deek, so I'm going to tell you. It's nobody else's business, you understand. It stays here."

I nodded.

"I told you I started out early on sharpening saws and going to lumber camps. It wasn't easy to make a buck, and in those days, a person had to be tough. Not like today. You either worked hard or you didn't eat. Well, I was young enough to work twelve, fourteen hours a day—it didn't matter as long as I made money. Then, with learning machine work, I had it pretty good. People knew I could build them anything they wanted. So when Prohibition came, I made up a few stills for some boys." I heard a younger voice rise. "Why, one was made to sink in the swamps when the government boys came and float back up when they left." He giggled, and I smiled with a chuckle—the story I had heard about the stills was true. "Anyway, I was asked to run the truck a few times to Minneapolis and got pretty good at it until I was running back and forth to Minneapolis most of the time. There was always this one place on Washington Street where I would unload, get some sleep, and head back. I met some interesting people over there. Some folks would just as soon put a knife in your back as look at you. But there were others, too.

Good folks that took an interest in me. They must have known that I couldn't read but back then, city folks just guessed it was because I was from a town in the woods they never heard of. They never knew why or cared. They just took it upon themselves to see that I learned about things—lots of things." Archie paused slightly, taking the kind of breath I take before singing—a quick catch breath—then recited,

> *Whenas in silks my Julia goes*
> *Then, then methinks how sweetly flows*
> *That liquefaction of her clothes.*
> *Next, when I cast mine eyes and see*
> *That brave vibration each way free;*
> *O how that glittering taketh me!*

I laughed noisily, shaking my head—the incongruity of hearing Robert Herrick bounce off grinders, lathes, anvils, an air compressor, benches, and whatnot in a machine shop. It was glorious and real, shiny like newly turned stock, alive like cherry wood.

I could not have been more stunned, but not over Archie's recitation of sixteenth-century poetry, although I was amazed at that. I was stunned because the recitation fit Archie—that for reasons of passion and life, Archie's shop and his wide suspenders and grease-stained hat dovetailed with Herrick's lilting poem.

"There's lots more I learned from people all over the place," Archie said excitedly. "The lucky thing about leaving school, Deek, was I got to pick my teachers."

Archie carefully picked up his stack of drawings from the bench top and put them in a box under the bench.

"Well, Deek," Archie said, slowly lifting himself from the oak chair, "what about that Jeep of yours? No sense having something if you can't use it."

For the next hour or so we talked about the Jeep. Unlike earlier in the day, Archie dug into the project using the word "we" whenever he referred to fixing this or that. He questioned my desire to restore the Jeep, reminding me that the wild north woods would show no mercy. "One trip up the Bissel grade will take off any shine you put on it," he said, referring to an abandoned railroad bed that ran north to Winter. "No sense wasting your money on looks." Agreeing that the real purpose of the Jeep was to get into and, more important, out of the wilds, we decided to have the engine rebuilt at a professional shop. "We need to spend our time and your money on getting the rest of it in top-notch condition," he said emphasizing the word "your." "You're going to need a lot of new parts, I hope you know that."

I thought he was pulling my leg when he told me that I could get them at Sears, but sure enough, when I inquired, they had a catalog devoted to old Jeeps.

Our plans laid out for the Jeep project, I left Archie standing by his musky wash-up barrel and, tucking Jason's Conestoga wagon safely under my arm, I headed for the Jeep. I would limp it home, then to the garage, where its engine would be pulled and rebuilt.

# 11 · The Cabin

*I hear America singing, the varied carols I hear,*
*Those of mechanics,*
*each one singing his as it should be*
*blithe and strong . . .*

Walt Whitman, *I Hear America Singing*, 1860

"Now what?" I asked Archie as I slid the transmission out from under the Jeep, which sat without engine or wheels high on four sturdy jack stands in Archie's shop.

"What do you mean, what?" Archie responded. "Put it in your car, take it home, and rebuild it. You got the parts I told you to order, didn't you?"

"Came in two days ago, they're down at Sears."

"Well, go get them and get on with it."

"Archie, I've never rebuilt a transmission before. I understand they're pretty complicated."

"Not this kind, Deek. They're simple—just be careful you put it together the same way you take it apart. Except," he added with a chuckle, "don't forget to trade the old parts with the new ones."

Archie's poignant disclosure about his past had raised our friendship to a level of innocence, more like that found between two young men in their late teens or early twenties as opposed to two grown men. No longer were we bound to the manners and protocols that had interfered with spontaneity in the early part of our friendship. I suppose we both let our boys out of their proverbial pen. By no means had Archie's sarcasm abated, far from it. He continued to use "teacher," never without a barb or two to make it stick. But never mind, I heard it differently now that I knew and he knew that I knew the source of it. There was no strain or reason for me to be other than pleased at the odd attention. I had taken to retaliating against his attacks now and then by referring to him as "Arch" or when more armament was needed, "old man," which always raised his hackles. We played work, not to say that tolerances weren't adhered to or welds weren't tightly done; rather, our work lightened.

I took a few minutes to clean up the case and dump the oil.

"Pretty classy oil, Archie. It's sprinkled with gold dust," I quipped.

"More like brass dust from the synchronizing gears. They're probably worn to nothing."

I put the transmission in the trunk of my car, where it joined all sorts of other Jeep parts and related stuff. The Jeep project had taken over my life.

Restoring, or more aptly put, getting the Jeep on the road and adapting it to Archie's woods, was into the second week. Before towing it to Archie's shop, it had, under its own power, limped to the fellow who I contracted to pull, rebuild, and replace the engine along with installing a new clutch and pressure plate. The rest was up to Archie and me and there was a lot of *rest* to deal with.

Front end, rear end, drive shaft, wheel bearings, steering box, brakes, electrical system, transmission, and transfer case all needed attention, parts, and money. My visits to Sears increased, as did a fairly steady stream of phone calls to Whitney's, an auto parts specialty store out of Chicago. What I couldn't buy or afford, like the worm gear in the steering box, Archie made.

Rather than rebuild the transmission in my garage, I took it directly from my car trunk to the floor in the family room, upon which I had laid a good padding of newspapers—why not make rebuilding the Jeep into a family affair? After removing a few bolts, the cover came free with just a bit of reluctance. After all, the case had probably never been opened since the day it was closed up at the Jeep plant in Toledo, Ohio. As Archie had foretold, the inside of the transmission was a simple enough affair, and everything looked to be in good shape with the exception of the brass synchronizing gears, the teeth of which were, as Archie suggested, worn to nubbins. I carefully took the gear train apart, replaced the worn gears, and popped it all back together in about two hours' time, which included a cup of hot chocolate and occasionally wiping grease off of our dachshund's nose. Kim and Jason made quick use of the old gears, adding them to the collection of odds and ends they squirreled away.

"You know, Deek," Archie said during the final days of working on the Jeep, "there's one more thing we need to add to this machine of yours—a winch. And I think I have just the right parts in that shed out there." I followed.

When Archie first took me on a tour of his shop complex over a year ago, he included only two of three shacks that lined the lane leading from his house to what I likened to a model of an industrial complex. I was about to see what was in that third shack. I waited patiently as Archie used the same drama he always used when opening a padlock. "Come in here," Archie commanded after opening the door and turning on a light. "We ought to find a power takeoff or two that might fit your Jeep." It was by no means a very large shack, more like a one stall garage, but typical of Archie's layout, the laden shelves gave it the appearance of a warehouse, in this case, a warehouse for antique car parts. "Let's see now, where might that be," Archie said, more to himself than to me. Moving what appeared to be transmissions, he declared, "I thought I had one of these. Here, Deek, a power takeoff that should bolt right up to the transfer case."

"Archie, where in the world did you get all this stuff?" I marveled once more at what he had accumulated.

"Here and there. Oh, come over here, Deek," Archie said excitedly. "Go ahead—pick one out, something catchy." I hesitated. "No, Deek, pick one out."

I reached into an old wooden, fingerjointed box that was full of old gearshift knobs as if I had been invited by Long John Silver himself to dip into a pirate's chest of gold, and these were worth every bit as much. I chose a marbled glass hefty knob. "How about this one?" I asked.

"Good choice. It's off of a Peerless. Good car. Now let's get out of here before I give too much away."

A heavy coat of red enamel, a tow to have the engine installed, a few adjustments, and my Jeep was like, if not better than, new. In a matter of a few weeks, give or take a few days away from the shop, twice-a-day tea breaks at the Indianhead, and jaunts up to the woods, the Jeep had undergone a radical transformation from shambles to purposeful dignity.

"Well, I guess it's time to take that Jeep up to my woods and give it a try," Archie said a few days after I had paraded my Jeep about town. With the windshield lowered and the top down, I played Jeep Man for Kim and Jason and their numerous neighborhood friends. A few of their parents joined in to boot. My good neighbor, Leonard Boss, was so delighted with the Jeep that he came by with two brand-new high-backed white vinyl car seats that he had bought to restore a car he had been working on but abandoned. To any Jeep aficionado, installing these seats in a Jeep was akin to blasphemy, but, in favor of Leonard and my tender back, I installed them in less than an hour. "Nice furniture," was Archie's sarcastic response.

"They're comfortable. Are you ready to go?"

"You have a good pair of boots?"

"Not with me. Why?"

"Never mind, I have an extra pair you can borrow. You never know when you're going to need them."

The first day I spent in Archie's shop came to mind, when I painted the lathe. "I have a feeling that you're setting me up. What's on your mind, Arch?"

"You keep up with that 'Arch' business and you'll need more than boots to get you out of a mess."

I let it drop.

We drove past the iron gate guarding the lane that went to Archie's cabin and headed directly to Harry's place, where we took a turn north along Grass Road. "Head this way," Archie commanded, pointing to a lane just north of the one leading to Harry's airplane hangar. The day was overcast, a light gray sky giving the woods a flattened, two-dimensional look. Once past the northern edge of the runway, Archie pointed south. The Jeep seemed to float through the knee-high grass. Archie cautioned me to stay fairly close to the runway's edge to avoid a plantation of white spruce and red pine seedlings that he and Harry had planted a year ago. I assumed that we were heading to Stoney Creek where, Archie had told me, a hermit lived in a tar-papered shack. I hoped that I would finally get to meet the old man. But Archie had different plans.

"Okay, Deek, let's head west. We'll come to a road, then figure on where to go from there."

As I turned, I could feel the heavily lugged tires dig into ever softening grassy ground. I stopped, dropped the transfer case into low range, and shifted the transmission into second gear. This combination gave the Jeep incredible traction. To no avail. The further I went, the deeper the tires buried themselves in soft swampy land completely hidden by the tall yellow grass. Going into reverse just dug us deeper. The Jeep bogged down in mud up to its axles. Dirty water began oozing up through holes in the floorboard. Trees were too far away for either the front or rear winch cable to reach. Archie's measurement was perfect—the Jeep was hopelessly mired.

"I thought that you knew these woods."

"I do, every inch."

"Then why are we sitting here?" I asked angrily.

"I thought that you said your Jeep could go anywhere. Well, Deek, this is anywhere and it didn't seem to get through it."

"Now what?"

"Well, now Deek, unless you have a mighty sized grappling hook, it looks like you just might need a tow. If you need to get out, the boots are in the back. You wait here. I'll be back," he said, as if I could go anywhere.

"Where are you going?"

"Back to my cabin, it's only a half mile. The Weasel will pull that Jeep of yours out of the fix you got it in. Now you wait here and enjoy yourself. If you're lucky, you might catch sight of the hermit."

Guided by experienced eyes, his calf-high boots found patches of terra firma like stepping stones through a stream and soon he disappeared from sight. I turned off the ignition, smiled at my folly and Archie's ways, and let the wonders of the north woods take over. Peace was in these woods but it never came easily to me. Sitting in the Jeep, my mind tried to get me onto one thought or another from its random list of this and that until I put a stop to it. I didn't want to think, I wanted to sense, and that meant closing off my mind and giving over to the woods itself. And so I did until my ears, which had become accustomed to rustles, creaks, swishing, gurgling, and unknown timbres of the woods, were touched by the unmistakable sound of a human.

Enthroned behind the big, black steering wheel, grinning like the Cheshire Cat, Archie was making his way to me in his beloved Weasel. Knowing exactly where the hidden swampy land began and firm ground ended, he turned, stopped, and backed up to about thirty feet behind the rear of my Jeep. Lifting

a heavy oak plank from the floor at the back of the old, modified fire engine, he pulled out a hefty steel cable and said,
"Here, come and get this." Knee-deep in mud, which found its
way over the top of my borrowed boots, I hooked the cable to
the back of my Jeep, which the triumphant Weasel easily
extracted from the mud.

I couldn't help but laugh at myself as I followed him back to
his cabin to drop off the Weasel. "Well, there you have it. Keep
that mud in mind whenever you think that Jeep will take you
places you have no right being." In a more serious tone, he
added, "Now, Deek, you're from back east, where getting stuck
or broke down is no more trouble than picking up a phone. Out
here, getting lost or breaking down could cost you your life. Now
let's see if that Jeep of yours can get us home."

It was a good lesson, one that I kept with me whenever I ventured onto old lumber roads. When we got back to town, Archie
said, "Lillian was wondering if you could stop by for a cup of tea
before going on home."

"Of course, is there something wrong?"

"Nope, she just wants you to stop by."

"I'd love to."

Lillian welcomed me but, before offering me a place at the
table, admonished, "I think you had better wash your hands."
Leading me to the kitchen sink, she added, "I don't trust that
barrel of awful water that Archie uses out in the shop. You, too,
Archie." Archie was already on his way to the basement to
wash up.

As I approached the table, I noticed three place settings neatly arranged with the feeling of formality. After serving tea and
some homemade apple pie, Lillian sat, looked at Archie, then at

me and said, "Archie and I would like it if you and your family could come up to the cabin tomorrow." I graciously accepted the rather formal invitation and asked what time they would be expecting us. "We think around one-thirty would be nice," answered Lillian. We shared some small talk, finished our tea and pie, and I was on my way home all in less than fifteen minutes.

In all of the times that I had been to Archie's woods, I had not once gotten even a glimpse inside of Archie's cabin, which remained a mystery to me. More than once I was tempted to ask Archie about it but never did. Now that Lillian had invited my family to *the cabin*, I reasoned that, unlike Archie's woods, it was Lillian's cabin. Like the shop was his and the house hers. Without Lillian, the cabin was off limits, perhaps even out of sight.

My family's first visit to the cabin was exciting and memorable. We packed the car with all of those things that young parents need to cart along with two young kids: food, games, change of clothes, Wet Ones, a few books, candy, an assortment of toys. The word "Weasel" had found its way into lunch and dinner conversations and, I'm sure, into the childhood fantasies of Kim and Jason. My family was finally going to get a firsthand look at all the what-for.

We drove along roads now entirely familiar to me as we headed north into the wild north woods. Driving through Archie's opened gate, we descended the curving lane leading to the cabin, and there it was. The Weasel. Proudly displayed in a prominent place, strategically parked, no doubt, by its proud creator in anticipation of our visit. My children's eyes widened. The shades covering the cabin windows were up, the windows open. Archie was sitting at the sturdy iron-framed picnic bench feeding chipmunks corn kernels from his flattened palm. The cautious creatures jumped for cover the minute I opened the car door.

The weather was spectacular. The pungent odor of rotting leaves and wood was softened by the mild smells of bark, sap, and late-flowering bushes. Daylight lit the colored leaves of the fall woods to resplendence.

"Well, look what the cat brought in," Archie said, approaching the car. "Come on over. Bring those kids of yours with you," Archie said, directing Bonnie and me to the picnic table. Within a few quiet minutes, the chipmunks were scurrying along the top of the picnic table, busily going from hand to hand gathering corn kernels into their ever-widening cheeks.

With the chipmunks fed and my children awed, Archie stood up. "Let's go into the cabin. Lillian has some eats waiting."

Even though the river was close by, Archie kept a wide-mouthed, cut-off wooden barrel full of water just outside the north wall of the cabin for his creatures to take a drink. On our way to the cabin, Kim wandered over to the barrel. Peeking over its rim, she asked Archie why he kept a small rectangular piece of wood floating in the clear water. He knelt by her side. "If you were a creature and fell in, wouldn't you want it there? Why, there would be no way out if they couldn't climb on board," he said, as if giving a lesson.

Satisfied by his answer, she pointed to an odd-looking water pump that sat next to the barrel. "Is that a pump like the pioneers used to have?"

"Yup, you want to see it work?" Archie said enthusiastically. Not waiting for an answer, he called to Lillian, who had yet to appear from inside the cabin. "Lillian, turn on the pump."

With that, a belt that led from an electric motor began turning a wheel that drove a gearbox, from which a cam raised two wooden slats connected to the top of the pump. Within a few seconds, the spout was gushing with clear, cold water. The pump sounded like it looked, very comical, drawing squeals of laughter from Kim and Jason, to whom Archie offered a tin cup filled with well water.

Lillian appeared at the cabin door. "Now, Archie, that's enough. Why don't you folks come inside?"

The cabin was spotless, quiet, and warm. There was a fresh, clean smell to the place. An old, well-used, heavily built, cast-iron lumber camp woodstove capable of taking three-foot-long, branch-size logs, sat in the middle of the north-facing wall. Sparsely furnished, the cabin had a double bed, a wooden table with four spindle-backed chairs, two stuffed easy chairs, and a small couch covered with a green woolen blanket with black stripes. Water came from a hand pump on the counter next to a sink. A propane-fired stove sat next to it, its gas tank hidden behind a wooded enclosure on the outside of the cabin's north wall. Acoustic tiles covered the ceiling.

The wood-paneled walls were stark, with the exception of a map of Archie and Harry's woods drawn to scale and detailed with every twist and turn of numerous trails. As I studied the map, Archie informed me, "Harry's son, Dick, drew the map. It's accurate, too. Did I tell you that Dick joined Harry and me surveying every inch of this land? It took us two years. See any familiar places, Deek?" Clearly marked, I recognized Grass Road, Beaver Pond, Harry's airstrip, and the winding Thornapple crowning the northern reaches of the woods.

While we were relaxing at the table, Archie quietly left the cabin to fire up the Weasel. Lured to the sound of the wondrous machine, we headed outdoors. "Well, c'mon kids, let's go," Archie said. Bonnie and I were excluded. This was Archie's time with our kids.

As our relationship grew, I saw Archie's demeanor with Kim and Jason evolve from friendly adult to kindly old man. Although he never admitted it openly, whenever Kim and Jason were around, Archie took on the unmistakable role of grandpa.

"You kids hold on tight," I cautioned them nervously as I lifted Kim, then Jason, to the high seats. "Archie, drive carefully." Spoken like a father.

Archie introduced Kim and Jason to white and yellow birch, aspen, basswood, cedar, black ash, tamarack, maple, cherry, and oak. They stopped by hemlock groves, gathered pine cones from Norway and white spruce. Hazelnuts filled their pockets.

When they returned to the cabin after an hour or so, the back of the Weasel was loaded with odd-shaped branches, various leaves, an assortment of beaver cuttings, colorful stones, the whitened bones of an unidentified small creature, and lichen shelves of all sizes and shapes.

"We got as far as Wolf Hill," Archie proclaimed as he parked the Weasel.

"Dad, did you know that Archie has a white wolf?" Kim asked in breathy excitement.

Looking at Archie, who was grinning like a bad boy, I responded, "Oh, yes, Kim, I know all about the white wolf."

Back inside the cabin, Archie talked reverently about all of the creatures that lived in his woods. Porcupines, skunks, grouse, deer, beaver, woodchuck, bear, owls, and eagles joined squirrels, chipmunks, foxes, and wolves to give the woods special meaning and a Dr. Doolittle–like personality to Archie. He told how in winter, he kept the feeding troughs that he had about his woods full of corn for the deer. "In cold weather when the temperature sits around minus-twenty for a week or two, why, Harry and I go into the woods to look for sleeping bears. At that temperature, there's always more frost on the trees around dens."

Showing the kids photographs of bygone days, Archie talked about the days when lumber was king. Although Archie's woods would probably never be bulldozed for housing developments as were the woods of my childhood, it did know the ravages of machinery. From railroad beds to logging roads, the north woods of Wisconsin still show the marks of the busy turn-of-the-century timber industry. To keep the woods vital and help overcome remnants of those tough days, each year Archie and Harry planted at least a thousand seedlings of mixed evergreens. The Leni-Lenape Indians would have been very proud.

As we drove back home that day, the kids had enough stuff in the trunk to last through a schoolyear of show-and-tell and the seeds of memories that would take root for a lifetime.

# 12 · The Elm Tree

**_Friendship is a sheltering tree._**
Samuel Taylor Coleridge, "Youth and Age," 1823

I stepped out of the soft yellow-lit chrome and mahogany–lined elevator to face a Louise Nevelson. I was visiting the Honeywell Corporation home office in Minneapolis on a fund-raising visit for the college. Nevelson's work was boxes within boxes, variously sized, each crammed with geometric shapes and found objects that took scrutiny to identify. Everything in and including the box itself was painted a flat black. Reflections and shadows were subtle. It took work to delineate detail. For an overview, I stood back as far as I could in the relatively narrow hallway. I leered at it from each of its sides and even crouched down on the floor to get a bottom-up view. It must have been a curious scene, I'm sure, to passersby.

Following my successful presentation, I came back to the Nevelson, where I stayed for the next half hour or so. The entire piece was made of wood placed so that the end grain projected forward. I recognized that a lot of the pieces included ends of two-by-fours and dowels of various diameters, but for the most part, it appeared that each piece was selected at random from some highly creative furnituremaker's scrap heap. Small dark crevices created by thousands of pieces of wood held mystery, as if lurking in these places were endless riches. There are no words to describe it, metaphor at its best can't bring the piece before anyone. It must be seen to be recognized.

The Nevelson sculpture was, in its entirety, a kingdom of thought. A kingdom where no words are necessary or even warranted, a place where abstraction stirs the pot of creative juices until, through some miraculous process, out pops an idea, a concept that, if one is skillful enough, can become something tangible, like a machine or a musical manuscript, or, in fact, the Nevelson I was looking at. I thought of Archie.

I left the Honeywell building, greeted by a warming sun. Spring in the north country was like no other. Mild, sunny, late April days were something to worship, which is what I did by driving slowly back to Ladysmith on a circuitous route that took me through the Blue Hills, a remote and beautiful spot just north and west of Ladysmith. It was Wednesday, three days before Archie and I had planned to cut down a dead elm tree in my backyard. Usually, I looked forward to Saturdays that included some tough physical work, especially when shared with Archie, but this weekend would be different. I planned to tell Archie that I was moving to Ohio, where I had accepted a faculty appointment at Muskingum College. Since I had received the appointment a few weeks earlier, I had kept it to myself and my family, waiting for the right moment to tell Archie, if there was a right moment. I suffered with the inevitable and knew that the moment I told him, our relationship would change, probably become memory, inactive. I worried about Archie's reaction, whether he would become withdrawn, or worse, feel deceived. During the course of the last year, I had noticed Archie slipping a bit, his memory less sharp. But I was concerned about myself as well. Over the course of four years, Archie had become my closest friend. This would not be easy for either of us.

We had stretched our Saturday morning shop work to include Saturday afternoons, bumming about in his pickup, prowling back roads in search of what Archie referred to as deals—old abandoned or nearly abandoned machinery that in Archie's eyes could be fixed up and sold for a tidy profit. He gave me lessons in making a deal, how never to expose your intentions with too much enthusiasm, lest the price rise, to play the person like a hooked fish until your quarry was tied down in the back of the pickup and heading for a new life back at the shop. Now and then we stopped in Rose's Bar, an out-of-the-way place that advertised its fried chicken with a sign that read, IF YOU'VE EVER HAD A BETTER PIECE OF CHICKEN THAN ROSE'S, YOU MUST BE A ROOSTER. Our meandering took us in ever widening circles from Ladysmith, even as far north as Cornucopia, a tired fishing village on the shore of Lake Superior, where he was reacquainted with a retired fisherman who remembered Archie as the "fellow who fixed the gearbox in my boat."

While we argued politics, Archie being far more conservative than I, our differences usually ended with laughter over the folly of being human. We discussed religion, but only on a comparative basis, as neither of us was bound to specific doctrine or theology. We made odd calculations like how many gallons of sap goes through any one tree in a lifetime.

"What kind of question's that?"

"No, I'm serious, Archie. How much sap?"

"What kind of tree?"

"Oak, you seem to like oak."

"Oak is heavy wood, weighs around seventy pounds a cubic foot. How high is that oak tree of yours?"

"Let's say a hundred feet."

"Big tree, Deek. Now I heard somewhere that a tree that big would give off about two hundred quarts of water a day. Now, not including winter when the sap's pretty much in the ground, I would say each year the tree gives off about thirty thousand quarts. How old's this tree you got stuck in your mind?"

"Fifty-three."

"Then my guess would be three hundred seventy-five thousand gallons. Does that sound about right?" Of course, I had no idea or any way of knowing whether his calculations were factual or fictitious, but that didn't matter, as it didn't in so many other conversations or arguments we got into. What did matter was talking and cajoling and figuring things out.

We never talked about music, the other half of my mental coin. Nevertheless, my friendship with Archie had a profound effect on the way I understood and performed music. Dominated by teachers who demanded adherence to the score, my musical education was classic in every sense, where one is taught to revere the written note as if Saint Augustine himself dictated melody and harmony. But since getting to know Archie, I treated the score more like Archie treated his drawings, as a guide to an end product that, I was delighted to discover, was in my hands, or ears, as the case may be, to finish. I likened my music making to cabinetmaking and machining, where each of the parts fits perfectly to create a whole, an idea, its own unique architecture. I reconciled myself to the notion that art and craft are too closely allied to draw a line between the two. All of this inevitably led to a change in my teaching—music became the vehicle for the student rather than the student becoming a vehicle for the music.

Saturday morning came quickly. Archie drove up my driveway ready to go. I stirred.

The large, majestic elm tree that sat on the edge of the half acre behind our house had succumbed to Dutch elm disease two years before. Even in its bare state, the power of the tree overcame any desire on my part to cut it down. In winter, its bare branches, out to their tiniest ends, gathered hoarfrost to give it an angelic appearance. In summer, the purple hues of the northern sunset slipped from limb to limb, twig to twig, creating a silhouette of quiet, resolved peace. The tree's death had been slow, and for the past few years, I gathered more and more branches in increasing size from the ground after each storm's blow. Each spring for the past five years, there were fewer and fewer buds, less and less life, until death halted its annual rebirth. With each passing storm, its dignity lessened as larger and larger pieces of its fragile architecture altered its form from graceful power to serene resignation. The time had come: The elm would have to be cut down.

Holding my half-filled cup of coffee, I greeted him. "You want some tea, Archie?"

"Nope, can't drink tea with a chainsaw in my hand." He hefted a large chainsaw from the bed of his pickup and headed around the corner of my house to the waiting elm.

"Deek, when you're done with that coffee of yours, get the Jeep. We need some extra insurance with this one. I have the rope."

I brought my Jeep from the garage into the backyard, where we attached a hundred-foot length of three-quarter-inch nylon line from a sturdy branch on the elm to the back of the Jeep. The extra insurance was so the tree fell on my land instead of on Jim Swanke's shrubs, cars, electric lines, garden implements, and the roof of his modern, one-story house.

Nudging the Jeep forward, the nylon line tightened. "That's enough, that Jeep of yours isn't going to pull down the tree on its own, no matter how good you think it is," Archie said with sardonic humor.

Archie's chainsaw came to life with the spitting rattle typical of a two-cycle engine. A puff of bluish smoke rose above his head and disappeared into the powder blue sky. "Now, Deek," Archie protested above the noise, "if I hit a nail or something in this tree, you are going to have to buy me a new chain. These neighborhood trees have more steel in them than skyscrapers." Archie's Homelite ate into the side of the tree that faced the back of my Jeep. With an angled cut, a sizable wedge of heavy, dead elm fell to the ground.

Thrown from the saw, fine chips of elm ran the length of Archie's left arm, clinging to his flannel shirt like tiny burrs. He switched off the saw and set it on the ground. "There were times when it would take two men slinging a saw a good part of an hour to take a tree like this down." Archie went on to reminisce about his younger days, something he did with increasing frequency. My mind was occupied by what I was to reveal to Archie later on in the morning, so I didn't pay particular attention to his story; rather, I nodded my head in recognition of this and that. By the time he finished, I had picked up the hefty wedge. "What is it you want with that?" he asked.

"I'm not sure. I like its shape."

"Well, Deek, you might as well put it on the scrap heap for kindling. You know elm burns pretty good, although it leaves lots of heavy ashes. Might as well use it in that stove of yours for winter heat," he concluded.

I felt a pang. "Good idea, Archie."

Rather than get back to felling the tree, we took a break, moving to our back deck, where Bonnie had some fresh-brewed coffee and tea waiting. Relaxed, Archie said, "This year, we're going to try to be in two parades on the same day, one over in Weyerhauser, then one up in Prentice. It means that the Fords and the old REO will have to move quick. You think they're up to it?"

"I suppose, Archie. At least during the first part of the summer," I answered truthfully, not willing to offer more.

Archie was referring to my driving the REO in parades throughout northern Wisconsin while Archie and Lillian drove their Fords. Each of the tiny towns surrounding Ladysmith celebrated holidays by parading their fire trucks, ambulances, marching bands, and homemade floats down their main streets. Antique cars were enticed to come to win any one of a number of trophies awarded in recognition of yesteryear. Archie and Lillian kept their numerous trophies on their fireplace mantel. The people of Weyerhauser, Bruce, Prentice, and Tony looked forward to seeing Archie's cars, especially the children, since it was Archie and Lillian's practice to toss individually wrapped candies to kids lining the parade way. Kim and Jason often joined in the fun, sitting in the rumble seat while Bonnie and I followed in the REO.

True to the advertisement that Archie had taped to the backside door of the REO's stall, the REO "floated" like a clipper ship with its large, flathead, straight, six-cylinder engine pushing close to four thousand pounds along the two-lane roads connecting the north woods communities. It steered like one, too, requiring a bit of muscle to turn the heavy, wooden, rather small-diameter steering wheel. The REO was not at all like the nimble Fords. It was big, very heavy, with iron fenders and massive wooden spoke wheels. I loved driving it, and I was going to miss it very much.

Our short break over, we walked back to the tree. Archie fired up the chainsaw and within a few minutes the honorable tree crashed with a *swoosh* and crackle to the ground, its upper branches harmlessly engulfing my Jeep. I walked among the branches of the felled elm touching twigs that no other had touched before. They were all brittle and easily cracked by my touch. I joined Archie with my small chainsaw, and between the two of us, we stripped the tree to its trunk, which we then cut into lengths ready for splitting and stacking. I found no pleasure in this latter chore, knowing full well that I wouldn't be the one burning them this winter.

Our job completed, I asked Archie to join me back at the deck. "I have something to talk with you about."

"Sounds serious, Deek. Don't tell me that Jeep of yours needs more work."

"It's not the Jeep," I offered as we sat down.

"Well then?" Archie looked at me seriously.

This was no time to beat around the bush so I came right out with it. "Archie, I've taken another job. We'll be moving to Ohio near the end of the summer."

"Is it a good job?" he asked quickly.

"Yes, Archie, it's a very good job."

We sat in silence, Archie resting his hands on bent knees. He cast his eyes downward, then stood and walked hunched over with his hands clasped behind his back to where the elm once stood. "What do you plan to leave for this tree, Deek? Isn't that something you need to do now that it's down?"

Rising from the stairs, I walked to where Archie was standing. "You're right. I'm afraid I didn't give it much thought."

"Nope, you didn't. Seems to me you didn't give all that much thought to moving those kids of yours away from here either. I don't think it's fair, Deek." Archie fell to silence then, raising his eyes to mine, he repeated, "I just don't think it's fair." He had tears in his eyes, as I did. Gathering up his strength Archie continued, "You know Deek, I'm a lot like that tree we just cut down."

"How's that, Archie?"

"Well, I've stayed in one place all my life. Put roots down here. Don't think it's all easy to stay in one place. People like to remember things the way they want. But I don't regret it. And just like this tree, I'm going to be gone soon. I've got a plot up on the hill in the cemetery behind the shop where I can keep an eye on things."

Quietly, he turned back to business at hand. "Now let's pack up. I got things to do."

Archie and I picked up our saws and walked toward my garage, where I set mine down on the bench then walked Archie to his truck where he set his saw and can of gas.

Getting into his truck, he closed the door and spoke to me out of the open window. "Deek, Lillian is planning a do up at the cabin tomorrow and would like you and Bonnie and the kids to come up."

"Sounds good to me, Archie. What time?"

"Some time after noon, Deek." He raised his truck window, started the engine, and backed out of my driveway.

# *Epilogue*

In 1979, interest rates had skyrocketed to eighteen percent plus. It was not the right time to sell a home. Waiting for the market to turn, I went to New Concord, Ohio, alone, where I lived in the basement of a dormitory, courtesy of Muskingum College, my new employer. During Thanksgiving, Christmas, Easter (spring break), and the summers of the two years I lived away, I returned to Ladysmith to be with my family and visit Archie. No matter how long my absence, the minute I walked into his shop, I was greeted with "Look at what the cat brought in." There was never any mention of my having left. We simply picked up where we left off—shop, woods, driving in parades.

House sale or not, I was not about to go a third year without my family. My good friend and dean, Dr. Dan Van Tassel, offered us a college-owned house rent-free until ours could be sold. We packed a U-Haul truck, added a trailer, filled the car, and headed south. The day before we left, I went to Archie's shop to say a final good-bye. But Archie would have none of it. His parting words were, "Take care of those kids of yours. When you get back, you'll know where to find me." No hug, no handshake, no taking my coveralls, which continued to hang on the back of the shop door. I just left with a "See you later."

Early the next morning, myself with Jason in the U-Haul truck with trailer attached, and Bonnie and Kim in the Volvo packed to the hilt, we turned from Route 8 to head south on 27. Parked near the intersection was Archie in his pickup. As I turned the corner, Archie pulled out in front of me, as if he were leading us out of town. He turned on the truck's blinkers and drove slowly along the road, keeping us at his pace until we reached the edge of town, then he turned west, as if freeing us to go on our way. He didn't wave or blow his horn. But he did turn on a siren that he had installed under the hood of his truck. Its wail faded as we drove on. It was the last sight I had of Archie Raasch.

In the years following, I wrote letters and called every month or so. Lillian responded to both but Archie had an aversion to phone conversations, especially long distance.

On April 3, 1987, I got a call from Lillian. Archie had died and Lillian asked if I would accompany her to the funeral. I immediately flew from Plattsburgh, New York, where I was working for the State University of New York, to Minneapolis, then by car to Ladysmith. After the burial, we sat at Lillian's kitchen table. She gave me Archie's gold pocket watch and silver fob. She told me that when Archie proposed to her, he showed her his hands and his small tool box. "This is all I have to offer," he said to her. They got married in Minneapolis with, according to Lillian, "a few people I never met until then."

Lillian died of cancer a year after Archie's passing.

In the course of writing this book, I visited Ladysmith after a ten-year absence. Currently owned by a relative, Archie's woods are intact, although, without Archie's constant attention, the trails are overgrown and, for the most part, impassable. Following Archie's death, Lillian sold his machines and tools to a fellow south of town. After Lillian's death, the neat yellow house and property were, according to Lillian's will, deeded to a local church. The household contents were sold at auction. The garage that held his antique cars was torn down along with the small buildings that held Archie's precious hoard of antique engines and car parts. The shop building was covered with aluminum siding. Archie's antique cars are scattered about the area, housed in garages of collectors. The Weasel, which has gone through three owners, is the prize of a young man who drives back roads "just for the fun of it." He refused my offer to buy the machine.

However sad I felt over the disposition of Archie and Lillian's material goods was more than offset by the legacy of Archie, which is alive and well. Paul Bloomberg, who runs the scrap metal yard in Prentice, remembers Archie as "the smartest person I ever knew. Boy he had a mind. A darned good machinist." Harry's son, Dick Pedersen, told me, "My dad and Archie never quarreled over who owned this or who owned that. They owned the woods together. I helped Archie restore his Model A's, and it was really hard to get Archie to buy any parts. He wanted to make everything. Sometimes he would work well past midnight in his shop making something that he could buy for ten dollars." The president of the Ladysmith National Bank, Bob Peterson, remembers Archie as a private person. "He was very difficult to get to know," Bob told me. "He would do anything for a friend. Few people knew or understood Archie. He was very complex. I liked the man." Lillian's sister, Alma Edming, who with her husband, Walter, ran a small manufacturing company, told me that Archie made all of their machinery. "He just looked at what we wanted to make, then made a machine to make it." When Walter died, Alma sold the business to a person in Arizona. When I called the company to request some photos of Archie's equipment, the president of the company denied my request on the grounds that she considered the machinery a trade secret. Archie would have been proud.

Archie remains in my mind as much a part of me as anyone in my life. Whether in my shop or my studio, Archie's presence is with me. A few years ago, for instance, I guest-conducted the Trenton (NJ) Symphony Orchestra in a performance of Howard Hanson's "The Song of Democracy," which is a setting of two poems by Walt Whitman. During the introduction, Hanson asks for a solo note from the horn that leads to a soft orchestral response. During rehearsal, I led the horn player through her solo measure, then brought in the orchestra as called for in the score. Then I stopped.

The note that the horn sounded had been ethereal, beautifully played, perfectly executed. I felt that I had cut it short. Too much control. Archie zipped through my head. *Let yourself flow with the weld.* Looking at the horn player, I said, "It's up to you, not me." I asked the orchestra to listen to her and to concentrate on that note. "Listen for the moment when it is right for you to respond. Don't count, don't measure, feel." They did, I did, and it was a glorious, artistically honest moment.

Seasoned machinists feel that moment, too. So do experienced furnituremakers, welders, sheet metal workers, glaziers—all people who produce with their hands know that moment. They know when to stop, when to yield to physical matter, when the material feels right through the motion of a tool or machine.

Within a fifty-mile radius of most people, there are craftsmen making the finest furniture, machining intricate pieces from blocks of steel, fashioning boxes, lamps, cabinets, model steam engines, and all sorts of gadgets. These are quiet people who judge quality by the way a thing is put together. They have enormous pride in what they do and how they do it, and while age does add a measure of quality to most work, young craftsmen are every bit as dedicated to being exact as their elders. Unfortunately, it is increasingly difficult for young craftsmen to discover and express their talents.

A picture of Archie standing proudly at his lathe has graced my studio or office ever since I left Ladysmith. Perhaps the incongruity of having a machinist displayed among pictures of composers and musicians attracts many to ask, "Is that your father or grandfather?"

"Oh, no," I usually respond, "that's Archie. He was a good friend of mine."